Praise for *The Opaque Conspiracy*

If you enjoy hard-hitting fiction that tugs at the heartstrings while delivering bad news, The Opaque Conspiracy is well worth reading. The story it tells of a couple who thought they had it good after decades of hard work building their careers, only to have it all yanked away by a shady bank and the greedy business scammers it enabled is not for the faint of heart. Through it all, Bonita, the narrator, retains her faith in herself and her husband, a retired general who was betrayed by those he believed in.

Honorable Theresa Speake | Former Director/Office of Economic Impact, U.S. Department of Energy

An intense, shocking story of business corruption that reads like it was ripped from the front pages. Author Grace Flores-Hughes tells the story of a successful couple unprepared for the massive deceit perpetrated on them by shady business executives linked to a prominent bank. A real page-turner that reveals the dark side of the business world—a milieu where financial institutions profit when companies stumble

Jerry Haar, PH.D. | Professor and Executive Director for the Americas College of Business Florida International University

This novel serves as a powerful and poignant reminder of the devastating effects of corporate greed and malfeasance on the lives of ordinary people.

Through the compelling and engaging narrative, readers are taken on a journey that explores a complex and intricate web of deception and corruption that leaves the protagonist and her husband mystified, disillusioned, and financially devastated. The author has done an excellent job of weaving together the various threads of the story, creating a gripping tale that is both informative and inspiring.

Despite the overwhelming adversity that the couple faces, the protagonist's resilience and determination shine through. The author portrays her as a strong and courageous woman who refuses to give up, even in the face of seemingly insurmountable obstacles. This book is a testament to the power of perseverance and the human spirit, and readers will be inspired by the protagonist's tenacity and courage.

I highly recommend this book to anyone interested in the themes of corporate greed, fraud, resilience, and love in the face of adversity. The author's adept narrative, combined with the significant and topical subjects it explores make it a must-read.

Martha Bodenheim | Resident of San Antonio, Texas

Few books are willing to tackle the subject of business corruption as unflinchingly as *The Opaque Conspiracy*. It's a story of a distinguished couple whose lives are forever altered by the chicanery of a bank and the schemers it supports. If you are a fan of thrillers or business books, this reads like a combination of both. I highly recommend adding it to your collection.

Debra Kube | Resident of Virginia

An unsettling but powerful novel that exposes the heart of darkness of modern business—the ability of corrupt practices to flourish when executives can profit from a company's misfortune as well as its success. In this well-written novel, Grace Flores-Hughes skillfully weaves the story of how the American dream can turn into a nightmare when a couple's prosperous life is destroyed by the machinations of a malevolent cabal of corrupt business executives. Through it all, Bonita, the narrator, retains her faith in herself and her husband, a retired general who was betrayed by those he believed in.

This is very exciting!!
Christian I. Martinez | Resident of Richmond, Virginia

"C.E." was the kind of man I once served under. A man who possessed common sense, decency, honesty and integrity. I am taken with the likes of "Bonita"….a woman of intelligence, grit, street smarts and keen insight. To read about their loss of property and reputation broke my heart. C.E. came from honor and trust but was overmatched by greed and deceit. This book is about all of it, and if you are like me, you'll find it very hard to put down. Part fast paced thriller and part exposé. And most of all a cautionary tale, especially for those without prior scar tissue from the business "school of hard knocks". The author offers, through her discovery and digging, a checklist of "do's and don'ts, and the dangers of swimming with sharks.
General Hal Hornburg | USAF, Retired

This novel describes a chain of events that add up to a terrible inhuman injustice against a man who honorably served his country as a three-star army general and one who worked very hard to build a small industrial company as its President and CEO.

Lt. General C.E. Levine started and managed a successful enterprise-until a bunch of white-collar crooks-designed and executed a master plan to use trickery and lies and destroy his perception of the financial reality surrounding his company.

The book represents a good study-case for management graduate schools, because it shows how external factors can destroy a good company. It also demonstrates that business leaders must be careful when presented with legal contractual documents by banks.

Banks are quick in offering loans to enterprises, but their executives can become corrupted- almost criminal towards well-meant individual clients. It is a warning to not trust many of the documents they fill your desk with. They can create a curtain that blocks the real intentions of their strategies.

Dr. Sergio Levin Kosberg, Ph.D | Retired Strategic Management Professor Universidad Autonoma del Estado de Morelos, Cuernavaca, Morelos Mexico

With The Opaque Conspiracy, Grace Flores-Hughes has written a novel that is both thrilling and heartbreaking. This is a story of how the American Dream can turn into a nightmare when powerful institutions and corrupt individuals conspire to destroy lives. But amidst the pain and suffering, there are moments of love and resilience that make this a book worth reading.

Glenn Hopper | Director, Eventus Advisory Group, and Bestselling Author of *Deep Finance*

The Opaque Conspiracy is a novel that will keep you on the edge of your seat from start to finish. This is a story of how the powerful can exploit the vulnerable and how the business world can be a ruthless and unforgiving place. But amidst the darkness, there are moments of beauty and grace that make this book a must-read.

Sanjay Jaybhay | Author of *Invest and Grow Rich*

Author Grace Flores-Hughes has written a novel that is both thrilling and thought-provoking. The Opaque Conspiracy is a story of how a corrupt business culture can destroy lives and how easily the American Dream can be stolen. But it's also a story of resilience and hope, and how even in the darkest of times, there are people who refuse to give up.

David Fuess | CEO, Henson Group

A page-turner of the highest order, The Opaque Conspiracy is a story of how the American Dream can turn into a nightmare when big business colludes with corrupt individuals. The characters are well-drawn and the plot is intricate and gripping. Author Grace Flores-Hughes has written a novel that will keep you guessing until the very end.

Shawn Johal | Business Growth Coach, Elevation Leaders, Bestselling Author of *The Happy Leader*

I couldn't put down The Opaque Conspiracy, which is a shocking and intense story of business corruption that reads like it was ripped from the headlines. Grace Flores-Hughes has done a masterful job of capturing the greed and ruthlessness of modern business culture.

Rick Orford | Co-Founder & Executive Producer at Travel Addicts Life, and Bestselling Author of *The Financially Independent Millennial*

I couldn't stop reading The Opaque Conspiracy, which is a true page-turner that grabs you from the first page and doesn't let go. The story of a couple who fall victim to a corrupt bank and its unscrupulous executives is a cautionary tale for anyone who thinks that business is all sunshine and roses.

Tamara Nall | CEO & Founder, The Leading Niche

One of the most powerful exposes of corrupt banking practices I have ever read. Although fictional, *The Opaque Conspiracy* reeks of reality, so to speak. Author Grace Flores-Hughes tells a story that shines a light on the ability of banks to profit not only when companies do well, but also when they are in distress. The action takes on a grim inevitability, as step by step a coterie of corrupt businessmen scheme to steal the benefits of the narrator's husband's hard work. Overall, a gripping read that—metaphorically speaking—grabs you by the throat and won't let go.

**Leonard Spearman, Jr. | Retired Senior Assistant,
Dept. of Energy and White House Deputy Associate**

The Opaque Conspiracy documents the theft of a successful American company on the precipice of enormous success. As the author demonstrates in case after case any consideration of ethics, or altruistic goals, are repeatedly sacrificed to the unbridled pursuit of an accretion of wealth and power for the perpetrators. This heinous behaviour was enabled by a banking entity--motivated by the perpetrators—to effect the takeover of the company not just its assets. Aside from their own material enhancement, these vermin have no ends, only the means of exercising their own will to power. This mind-set is reminiscent of the scene in the film *Molly's Game,* where after a late night poker session one of the key players--and consistent winners--says to Molly "You don't understand, I don't play poker just to win money, I play poker to destroy peoples' lives". This is the essence of *The Opaque Conspiracy:* clearly and unmistakably illustrating the dangers of so called business executives with no guiding ethics, enhanced by no respect for the law, and a willingness to bend the truth where convenient at the expense of ruining innocent lives. A must read!

**Lon Ratley | Former Daimler-Benz
Aerospace VP and Colonel, USAF (Ret.)**

THE
OPAQUE
CONSPIRACY

FINDING A WAY OUT OF
DESPAIR AND DESTRUCTION

GRACE
FLORES-HUGHES

FOR ALL OF THOSE THAT HAVE WOKEN UP IN
DARKNESS

"Yesterday is not
ours to recover, but
tomorrow is ours to
win or lose."
—Lyndon B. Johnson

ISBN **978-1-63735-225-0** (hcv)
ISBN **978-1-63735-223-6** (pbk)
ISBN **978-1-63735-224-3** (ebook)

Library of Congress Control Number: **2023906508**

Contents

Prologue

I took my stance, ball in the left hand, racket in the right, poised, almost holding my breath as I looked across the net at my opponent, a tall lanky blonde with a smug look on her face. Who was I? A petite, dark skinned 14-year-old with the strong features of my father's indigenous ancestors, the Garza's of Mexico. Only my mother's Spanish-Jewish background presented itself in my frizzy curly mophead, a characteristic foreign to my indigenous Garza relatives of Mexico. I had no smug look on my face; I must have looked panic-stricken. As I stood there motionless, my mother's words came into my head: "Bonita, no matter if you aren't accepted by others, or if you don't think you can win a single game, you stay in it and compete. Before you know it, you may just win." I took a deep breath, then slammed that ball across the net. My opponent, surprised at the sudden change in my demeanor, dove to reach it, but missed by an inch. My point!

I was born Mercedes Goyo Garza. But, on the day I was born, my maternal grandmother, Doña Lucia Goyo, whom I called Nanita, excitedly pronounced, "*Que niña tan bonita!*" The word *bonita* means pretty in Spanish. The name took! And when I married Carlos Ernesto Levine, better known as C.E., I took his last name and have been known as Bonita Levine ever since. I am about to tell you a kind of story that may elicit anger, bring a tear to your eye, and in the end, an expression of sadness mixed with joy.

A few years ago, my life as I knew it turned on a dime in a most devastating way. My husband C.E. Levine and I lost everything we worked for our whole lives: our finances, our reputation, our home, and everything in it. You name it, we lost it. We didn't lose these things because of a world-wide pandemic, or a fire that razed our home, or a natural disaster that wreaked havoc. We lost them because business circumstances threw both of our lives into a trap of devastating financial losses affecting both our professional and personal lives. The unforeseen set of business circumstances turned into a culmination of bad timing and bad decisions, ending in bad luck all around. All of it advanced by a well-orchestrated sinister mob, godless people. It felt at the time that an angel of darkness enveloped our lives and our souls, overpowering us while we stood helpless, unable to fend off the powerful *negative spirit.*

Losing a job is traumatic, no matter who you are or how you lost it. But losing a career and everything you worked for is a life-changing—life-threatening—experience. During America's Great Depression, many men ended their lives instead of facing their financial disastrous present and an even worse future. They jumped out of buildings, put guns to their heads, or slashed their wrists. Death seemed the best alternative to facing financial failure on a large scale and the new reality of a dark and uncertain world.

When C.E. lost the company he led and his job a few years ago, we both felt like the victims of the Great Depression. The circumstances behind C.E.'s losses and its fallout at first endangered our personal finances and later destroyed them along with the professional careers we both had built over decades. Even though C.E. and I found ourselves in a similar situation as some in the Great Depression, we soldiered on as best we could, holding on to each other for strength as we wobbled our way through depression and despair, and hoping somehow, some way, to return to the ordinary world we once lived. That did not happen; things got much worse.

I met my husband C.E. Levine more than 40 years earlier in an East Coast U.S. military installation and married him a few years later. Even though there was a generational difference in our ages, C.E. appeared and acted much younger than his years, adjusting well to my 1960's youthful experiences and attitudes. C.E. had a successful career in the U.S. Army, retiring as a three-star general. Afterward, he consulted for some of America's top corporations before becoming president and CEO of a small industrial company. In some ways, my professional career matched his. I served in various senior level positions in both the private and public sectors.

Our married life started blissfully. Like many Americans, we both earned two decent incomes, always paid our bills on time, and managed to squirrel away a modest amount for a rainy day. The sudden end of the largest portion of C.E.'s income drove us into a tailspin of absolute uncertainty and crippling fear. Suddenly, I found myself where I had to marshal my strength—steel my soul despite the anguish and fright pulling C.E. and me down. I can't say that a failure of my will to live did not creep in, an actual battle fought inside your heart and mind that can wreck you mentally and physically. At times I felt my soul was on extended credit, terrified that at any moment it would expire when I least expected it. But ultimately, I realized that blowing my brains out or taking a short step off a tall building was not the answer. I had a life to live, unpredictable as it seemed.

I took up tennis in high school, a game in which people of my ethnic background were not welcomed at the time. I loved the game and was determined to participate. Tennis is physically exhausting but calculative and highly competitive. It teaches many life lessons. How to figure out an opponent's moves and calculate how to move against them. Staying in the game until you exhaust and outmaneuver them gives you openings and an opportunity to score points and win, keeping your eye on the ball: game, set, and match. Those tennis skills came into play in the most important off-court event of my life—when C.E. and I lost everything.

For several years, I've tried to figure out how a relatively small company with questionable resources professed to pay only $3.4 million for my husband's company's assets, ending up with the entire company and all of its contracts worth millions, and reselling those contracts for almost $50 million without so much as bringing any other business to the table.

At the time of its asset sale, C.E.'s company was valued between $30 and $35 million. It had almost $50 million in pre-awarded contracts within reach and a pipeline of close to $150 million over five years. And yet, C.E.'s company's lender, a Connecticut-based bank, forced C.E. and his two officers to sell the assets of his company to a company literally formed overnight, while refusing to pay C.E. the severance left in his contract totaling almost $1.2 million. To find a place for those assets, the new owners formed a company and named it almost identically to C.E.'s former company, C.E. Inc. versus C.E. LLC. Was the name calculated to confuse the public that both companies were one and the same? Could this have been orchestrated by the new owners to take control of C.E.'s entire company, not just its assets, while not paying for its full value?

The formation of a new company is not unusual for mergers and acquisitions. What is remarkable is that this particular company didn't have the most essential mechanism required to bid for and be awarded federal contracts: a federally-assigned proprietary number of its own. These events, plus others you will read about later on, left C.E. with literally nothing. The domino effect eventually destroyed his good reputation and indirectly mine, not to mention our livelihood.

For years I was a tormented soul by the events, unable to sleep, tossing and turning, waking up in a cold sweat night after night. My anxiety level was an unending crescendo of stress. Nothing about my husband's company's asset sale made sense. But rather than get stuck in an endless cycle of fear, despair, and uncertainty, I went to work to find out the three most celebrative lessons of early education: who was involved, what really happened, and why it happened. I stayed in the game, keeping my eye on the ball, not knowing whether I could unveil the mystery and reveal the truth behind the company's asset sale. The words of my late mother, Lola Goyo, pushed me to find the truth. They echoed in my mind: "The hell with the *bolillos that don't want you to play tennis. Stay in the game and keep your eye on the ball. Before you know it, you may just beat 'em." And so, I stayed in the game and it served me well. I discovered there was far more to the story than what C.E. told me the day his company's assets were sold by its lender. (*The term *bolillo is general slang referencing white people that is used primarily in the southwest region of the U.S.—the name is based on a white Mexican/French bread.)*

I share this story for many reasons. The main one is that no matter how tough life seems, there is a Higher Being looking after all of us. After C.E. and I fell from the heights we had worked so hard to reach, I resorted to anger, fear, then downright despair. All three consumed me to a point where I no longer recognized myself. The once happy-go-lucky girl possessed with tough southwestern grit no longer existed. It took almost five years before I began to feel the rays of God's light shine upon me and my broken life, only to see that light go out again.

I am convinced that all humans will face a dark period at some time in their lives. In our case, I asked myself more than once: Is this God's way of putting the spotlight on us because we've been judged as not good enough human beings, or is it simply bad luck? There are too many unpunished bad people—we see and hear them every day—for me to believe we failed at being good people. C.E. and I are not saints, but we are compassionate people who have done our best to follow the Golden Rule. But in the real world, that does not always matter. There are people out there who will screw up your life at a moment's notice, for some other ungodly reason. It's how we handle the challenge that is the crux of this book, along with the warning to be on the lookout for the kind of wicked dealmakers that will drown their own mothers in quicksand for a fast buck.

Read along as I relive it in my own words.

A word of advice: When you witness a friend or associate who might have been a victim of either unforeseen or calculated circumstances, do your best not to turn a deaf ear. Help them. Listen and show compassion. Who knows? *'There, but for the grace of God, go I….'*

Now, let me take you back to before my dark period began.

Chapter 1
A Once Happy Life

"Don't cry because it's over; smile because it happened." —Dr. Seuss

I married a quiet and reserved man who rarely expressed his innermost thoughts. Yet on a warm spring day several years ago, C.E. had a twinkle in his eye and the broadest smile I had ever witnessed, including the day he was promoted to his dream job—Director of the Joint Staff. That was an enormous responsibility requiring the command of thousands of military and civilian personnel.

Yet, on that day—post-retirement from the Army—it was a different time and a different day for the man, at times, I endearingly called, 'Levy.'

"Bonita, it looks like we may be well on our way," C.E. cheerfully announced. He paused long enough to catch his breath and continued assuredly, "We're having a great year! Looks like the company is on track to earning millions of dollars in pending federal contracts." He smiled and let loose an "Eehaaaa" of victory as he wrapped his strong arms around me and pulled me close. His bear hug enveloped my blade-thin shoulders and squeezed my chest so powerfully it briefly squished the air out of my lungs.

At that moment, as we fused together, almost like a single celebratory figurine you placed proudly on your mantle, a river of tears streamed down my face to form a steady drip onto my shirt collar. I couldn't remember the last time I had cried so joyfully. Maybe it was when I was accepted to one of the top Ivy League schools in the country or married C.E. I was so elated, and that moment with him was so memorable. I wished to store that happy feeling in my heart forever.

C.E.'s joy stemmed from the millions of pending new federal contracts that his company was in the process of receiving. It was an achievement that he and his Chief of Operations (COO), Pancho O'Grady, had worked so hard to accomplish in the three short years since founding the company. Our lives were poised to change forever—our financial future was secure. And so were the lives of Pancho and his family and the company's employees that C.E. had led for over five years: two years as President and CEO of the original company, Zee Industries Inc., and the remainder as President and CEO of its forerunner, the newly-formed company, C.E. Inc. Everyone's ship was about to come in!

As we held each other, I thought about C.E.'s good fortune, both in his military and business career. It seemed that just about everything he set out to do turned out better than either one of us expected. Like Midas, the mythical king of Greek Phrygia, just about everything C.E. touched turned into golden opportunities for us.

C.E. had a remarkably successful military career. At 49, he was one of the youngest Army flag officers to pin on three stars. His combat tour in Vietnam consisted of close contact with the enemy in a variety of high-level and dangerous missions. He was a highly decorated soldier, earning a Silver Star among many other military awards.

C.E. retired at a time when I was moving fast in my own career. I became one of the highest senior level appointees in the government, leading a major domestic agency that required Senate confirmation. I was the first woman to oversee this small but critical federal agency. No wife of an active Army General Officer had ever been nominated to such a high level in the federal government. The military had a policy that its active military members should not be involved in political affairs, and indirectly that included spouses. My nomination and eventual confirmation broke all military protocol of that period. It set the beginning of new standards for extended family members who were professionals in their own right.

C.E.'s decision to retire early from the Army was admirable at best. He was determined to support me in my political career. A maverick personified, he had no qualms and quickly transitioned from the military to civilian life, exchanging his military uniform replete with 'gongs' (his medals and decorations) for a traditional business-style pinstriped suit. If he ever looked back and regretted his early retirement decision, he did it alone. A quiet man without comment, he does not dwell in the past and lives in the present and future.

Several companies came calling after he retired, but C.E. chose a mid-size million-dollar tech company for the transition, until he determined or decided what he specifically wanted to pursue in the next phase of his life. His senior vice-president's position earned him a generous salary, and we purchased a large brick townhome in the northwest part of Washington, D.C. The roomy, 4600-square-feet, four-level townhome was the first home we owned after years of living in military base housing.

Our home was strategically located on the corner of a street that invited sunshine year-round to the two rooms where we spent most of our time, the living and kitchen areas. But it was the uniquely designed brick patio that sold us. It was secluded, with an enchanting landscape designed by its previous owner. The geographic location was another attractive feature. It only took about 20 minutes to either reach downtown Washington, D.C., or the two country clubs we frequented. We loved the house. It was special because it was the first home we could purchase with our hard-earned money. Our neighborhood of townhomes was modeled after an English-style residential mews setting. Its narrow tree-lined streets and unique architectural designs were named after English noblemen and royal titles. Most of our neighbors were retired military working on their second careers, much like C.E. The military setting of the past carried on into our new civilian lives, where the fellowship of trust, camaraderie, and entertainment continued.

Our name appeared in the town's Social Register, along with all those who made it through their parent's money or through hard work or other inventive forms. Inclusion meant you had arrived!

We earned enough money between my salary and C.E.'s Army retirement and his salary as a Senior Vice President to make our home comfortable, invest some money, and travel. And to help family members and support some local and national charities, including helping a five-member family that lost their entire home in a fire.

After a couple of years at the tech company, C.E. became restless. He wanted out of a company that did not venture from its day-to-day mission of 'selling paper,' as he called it. The company pursued contracts that were extra staff work for the various armed services branches. But he wanted to find something more challenging and—more importantly to him—to become his own boss.

My four-year term presidential appointment was ending by this time. I was ready to do something else as well. The timing for us to change careers couldn't have been more propitious. We were at a new threshold of our lives, still young and excited about what we could build together. Both of us had a wealth of knowledge about the federal government's inner workings, domestically and internationally. So, we formed a consulting company using our experience and expertise to advise other companies.

As we established our company, we found our names (more C.E. the three-star general than me, a former political appointee) had significant credibility. Our income increased as we continued to build C.E.'s profile in the world of consulting and corporate boards. I found my role as the company's social planner, keeping the books, scheduling meetings and dinner events, and planning travel for us both. That role was surprisingly rewarding, albeit significantly different from my previous career, where I led over 100 personnel and oversaw a federal budget of well over sixty million dollars. We were building something together. C.E. was on the board of five major corporations and consulted for an equal number of other companies.

One highlight of this period was our financial ability to join a major golf tournament in Hawaii, at the invitation of a dear friend who was one of the leading creators in Hollywood. We went to Hawaii for a week's worth of golf and sun. We made this trek for eight years and made friends with many top creative figures of the entertainment industry, the heads of some of the top television networks and record companies, the producers and directors of some of Hollywood's top movies and television shows, as well as many famous stage and screen actors. Also, included in the mix of golfers were some of America's wealthiest families who turned out better golfers than anyone of us, some of whom we call our friends to this day. The list went on and on. One of my favorites was a well-known television producer, who had been married to a leading actress in a popular and award-winning television series. He was the past chairman of one of the top television networks. What an extraordinary mind and quiet charm that man possessed. He was one of the most fascinating people I ever met. A true gentleman in every sense. For some reason or another, we were assigned seats next to each other at most of the tournament's dinner events held year after year. Needless, to say, we found each other interesting and before long the flirting began, which led to us becoming enchanted with one another. I was flattered that such a famous and talented man took interest in this girl with roots far different from his impressive pedigree. But that was about it. I was spoken for, and he, being single at the time, was free to let his imagination wander.

Money was pouring in. At the advice and insistence of friends, we invested a portion of our newfound wealth in a parcel of land. I had a particular desire for a place on the water because it reminded me of the Pacific Ocean near where I grew up. But C.E. longed for the natural woods that reminded him of his home in upstate New York. He won the toss.

We were fortunate to find about 50 acres of wooded area in the Shenandoah Mountain foothills. At first, we thought of using the land as an investment and nothing more. But the more we traveled to our property, the more we thought about building a small home for weekends. We cleared at least half the land to make our dream weekend country retreat, a sprawling ranch-style house that sat atop a small ridge. We called it 'Martini Ridge' since C.E. and his friends enjoyed sipping James Bond's favorite cocktail drink. It was our small slice of heaven. And heavenly it was. We were gifted with a magical view of the stars that twinkled like diamonds across the dark night blanket of a vast Virginia sky. Large oak and walnut trees protected our property from public view. Our pear-shaped swimming pool faced a large mountain, where Confederate and Union soldiers had clashed. Its old-growth trees now watched over their ghosts and spread a palette of colors before us every autumn.

We were well on our way to earning more than we ever had and investing in future retirement. Our life was happy and prosperous. There was nothing we could foresee that would interrupt our trajectory. Then one of C.E.'s business associates recommended he sit on the corporate board of a small industrial company. He agreed. What happened based on that decision is an unbelievable story.

Chapter 2

The Selling of a Jewel for Next to Nothing

> "I sincerely believe that banking establishments are more dangerous than standing armies and that the principle of spending money to be paid by posterity, under the name of funding, is but swindling futurity on a large scale." —Thomas Jefferson

In the early 2000s, C.E. was selected to serve on the board of a small company located in Delaware. Formed in the 1970s, Zee Industries Inc. was a small, public-traded industrial company. Its sales, earned from contracts awarded chiefly by the federal government, were mediocre but consistent. Yet, C.E. wasn't keen about sitting on the board of a small industrial company with a questionable future. He was particularly skeptical about the future purchasing potential of its products by the military, the company's sole customer. He was even more doubtful about the company's ability to grow and increase its revenue enough to stay in business. But his terms on a couple of other boards that he sat on were about to end, so he began to reconsider. Also, the company had a couple of products that he thought had promise, which influenced his decision to accept the board membership.

One of the company's key products was a sophisticated piece of aviation equipment designed to enhance the military's survivability, something that the federal government needed. C.E. believed this device could determine the company's future.

C.E. should have listened to his instincts despite his interest in the product's potential. After a few months on the board, he learned that Zee Industries, Inc. had severe underlying management problems, mostly related to personnel. As time went on, the executive management team's problems multiplied, prompting C.E. and the other board members to become concerned and push for more information. Their concerns were justified. The company's leadership soon became the focus of a federal investigation. Both the company's CEO and COO were fired and eventually imprisoned for fraud. In the aftermath, and after a nationwide search for a CEO and president, the company's board selected C.E. to head the company.

With management and leadership experience, most of us think we can change a company's direction to suit our leadership style which, once supported by a diverse and equally-treated workforce, will lead to more gains than losses. C.E. was no different. He felt a calling to lead the company, which he thought had the potential to thrive if it shed the corrupt shell of its past and moved forward under capable management and a dedicated workforce.

For two years, the company puffed and sputtered as it tried to recover from the fallout caused by the imprisonment of its two principal officers. Finally, its lender, a small bank located in the northeast part of the country, led the company to file for Chapter Eleven bankruptcy. The bankruptcy resulted in the company eliminating its board of directors and publicly-held shareholders. This caused the board members, including C.E. and the company's investors, to lose their stock premiums. It was a dramatic and terrible turn of events. Both C.E. and I had risked all our life savings to purchase the company's stock when C.E. became its president and CEO. We lost it all in the Chapter Eleven bankruptcy.

In conversations between C.E. and the bank before the company filed for Chapter Eleven, the bank's representative stressed that the shareholders were risk-takers, and that being losers in the Chapter Eleven proceedings was unfortunate but a risk they accepted when they acquired the company's stock. However, as the bankruptcy filing progressed, it became clear that eliminating the 6000-plus shareholders, including C.E., was a 'must succeed move' for the bank's benefit. After the company emerged from bankruptcy, its lender, the Connecticut-based bank, offered the three officers of C.E.'s new company the majority percentage of the common stock, while the bank would own only a small percentage of the common stock, but one hundred percent of the preferred stock. This meant that the bank controlled the company and its finances. They, and only they, had access to the brakes and the throttle of the company when it came to funding their operation. In other words, by being the lender of operating capital for the emerging company, the bank set itself up to be a winner no matter how the new company fared business-wise. By establishing itself as the only lender of operating capital, the bank had its foot on the gas pedal—or the brakes—for the funding necessary for successful business operations. Their control resulted in money not being there on time to purchase raw materials required to keep operations running for three years, while their continued control prevented smooth business growth. Yet, even with that burden imposed by the bank, the emerging company, renamed C.E. Inc., grew and developed an enviable backlog of work under C.E.'s leadership. Was it possible that the bank had different and much more ominous plans for the emerging company and its officers at the outset?

After the old company, Zee Industries, Inc., filed for bankruptcy, the bank made big promises to C.E. The bank would fund the old company out of Chapter Eleven and continue as the lender to a new company with him as the president and CEO. It all sounded good. C.E. went along with the bank's encouragement and promises. When the bank offered to help jump-start the new company following the old company's demise, it might have been wise for C.E. to hire an attorney to examine his contract as the new company's president and CEO. C.E. might have also been wise to hire a corporate lawyer on behalf of the new company to examine its relationship with the bank, to understand how it affected its three management officers and employees. He didn't do any of that because he trusted the bank to support him in growing a business that had a proven profit-making capability and an enviable market base.

Consequently, his trust in the bank and belief in its promises cost both of us dearly.

After exiting Chapter Eleven as a new company, C.E. moved quickly to continue developing the products with the most potential and to expand its advanced aviation equipment. C.E. made only a handful of personnel changes in the initial process but added two critical hires. One was Pancho O'Grady as the COO. Pancho was a Naval Academy graduate and retired Navy Commander. He came highly recommended by a family friend, which sealed Pancho's hiring. For the Chief Financial Officer (CFO), C.E. chose Judith Wurm, a former bookkeeper. According to C.E., Judith showed capability he thought hadn't been realized by the former company's leadership. Also, Judith and C.E. had a bond in that they were both New York natives, born in the leafy town of Bedford. He wanted to allow Judith to show her talent beyond bookkeeping. This was not a new revelation from C.E. He supported women's rights during his military and civilian career by hiring and promoting women in the workforce. C.E. was the first flag officer to hire a female executive officer for his immediate staff. When she first came to C.E.'s attention, Captain Dulce St Thomas was working as an intelligence officer. After Dulce was hired, she broke the military glass ceiling and the informal rule that only men served as executive officers to General Officers. C.E. was impressed with Judith Wurm's potential, as he had been impressed with Dulce's potential twenty years earlier.

While hiring Pancho and Judith as his senior management team members, C.E. made a costly decision. He gave Pancho and Judith 33 percent ownership each to match his. When I learned about his decision, I warned him this arrangement might bite him in the ass one day. C.E. insisted he wanted them to get their fair share if the company was ever sold. I had my reservations and questioned his decision: "What if the bank decides to sell the company, and you oppose the sale, but Pancho and Judith agree?" Before C.E. could respond, I said: "You realize that Pancho and Judith can override your decision because they'll have the majority vote if they pair together." C.E. looked perplexed and shot back: "That won't happen, Bonita. Where do you come up with such poppycock, anyway?" C.E. always saw the best in people. The thought that his two closest business advisors would turn on him never entered his mind.

My words eventually proved prophetic. But, before that, the new company started winning federal contracts almost immediately. C.E. weeded out some of the troublesome staff and brought in replacements who helped the company grow sales and productivity. C.E. Inc. was off and running, creating quality products by a happy team proud of what they were producing and proud of who they were working for. Soon, the company had close to $50 million in pending federal contracts.

It seemed from the start that everyone associated with C.E.'s company appreciated its value and potential— except the company's lender and preferred stockholder, the bank. The bank's representatives didn't seem to understand, or want to understand, the products or their contribution to the company's profit, which benefited them.

The arrangement between the bank and the company wasn't without concern for C.E. and his management team. The bank provided working capital to the company, but as a 'pay-as-you-go' equity line disbursed at the bank's discretion. Since the bank was the preferred stock shareholder of the company, while C.E., Pancho, and Judith were merely common stock shareholders, the bank controlled the company.

From the start, the bank would lend one day but not on another without explanation, delaying funding at a whim. The delays crippled the company, preventing it from purchasing the materials to produce the products for its key customer, the federal government. Such throttling by the bank became the norm and, to add to the problem, the executives who had led C.E.'s company into and out of Chapter Eleven left the bank after the bankruptcy. Over four-and-a-half months, the bank switched its representative to the company three more times. The last one, Kane Hunter, a senior vice-president, was the only one to visit the company. He was in Maine, a long way from the bank's headquarters in Connecticut and even further from C.E.'s company in Delaware. In C.E.'s opinion, Hunter never seemed to understand the company's product demand from the federal government and showed little interest in doing so. According to C.E., Hunter immediately began choking the golden goose— the company—rather than feeding it. He pointed out the negatives in the company created mainly by circumstances and the bank's questionable funding decisions and put together a narrative that the company was on the verge of failure. It became a staged effort by the bank to take the company from the three officers, an effort that C.E. and Pancho didn't detect until it was too late.

The situation was that C.E. Inc.'s balance sheet, like many other companies across the country that did much of their business with the federal government, had changed for the worse. During the late 2000s, Congress and the president couldn't agree on a federal budget, causing the federal government to enter sequestration. That stopped all non-essential federal monies paid to vendors everywhere.

For C.E. and his company's team, government contracts were both a blessing and a curse. Under C.E.'s leadership, the company had close to $50 million in upcoming federal contracts, only to have those payments and awards slowed down and delayed, but not canceled, because of the sequestration. The government contracting officers responsible advised C.E. and his management team that the money for their programs and payments owed would be ready the minute the government reopened. So, the money was there—it would just take time for sequestration to lift before the funds could flow.

Still, Hunter told C.E. the bank wanted out of the commercial lending business, and they planned to stop providing working capital to the company. Hunter advised him to look for a buyer at $30 million. This surprised C.E. since there wasn't anything wrong with the company other than the impact of the sequestration, which would not last long. The company was paying its monthly loan payments. However, the bank still claimed it wanted to step away from funding working capital for C.E. Inc. It didn't seem to C.E. that the company was a priority for the bank. Their actions made little sense to him and Pancho.

One fall day in the late 2000s, the bank's law firm sent an overnight letter to C.E. advising him that no further advances on the company's line of credit would be forthcoming. The letter stated that the company had defaulted on a covenant in its financing and security agreement with the bank (the lender). The missed covenant—an interest payment to the bank—was caused by two decisive factors: one, the impact on cash flow from the federal government sequestration, and two, the abrupt seizure by the bank of a $3 million tax refund to the company after Hunter had reassured C.E. that the refund belonged to the company. When C.E. protested to his CFO, Judith Wurm, who was responsible for the refund's safekeeping in the company's bank account, she informed him that the bank was taking the money and there wasn't a damn thing he could do about it.

According to C.E., that was first tell-tale sign that Wurm was changing loyalty lanes from him to the bank. That refund would have bought much-needed raw materials and paid employees without furloughing them while waiting for federal monies to come in. But, more critically, this action caused the company to break its covenant with the bank. Thus, two events outside of C.E. Inc.'s control were used by the bank to put the company in default. Banks typically allow 60-90 days to catch up before foreclosing on properties, and C.E.'s expectation was no different. The company had begun to catch up. Although the start was slow and the company's balance sheet wasn't in the best shape, it was current with its loan payments to the bank. Yet the bank chose to ignore this and moved from selling the entire company for $30M to divesting the company as a distressed entity, selling its assets for a mere $3.4 million.

Shortly after receiving the bank's missive, C.E. was contacted by a reputable company located in the northeast. The company's president explained that one of his clients, a firm with revenue in the low billions, was looking to acquire a minority, majority, or 100 percent interest in C.E. Inc. based on its success as a world leader in aviation equipment. C.E. and his management team would continue to run the company. C.E. excitedly discussed the offer with the bank. Rather than pursue this intriguing proposal (one for the entire company and not just assets), the bank, which was the seller, ignored the offer and, from that day forward, put an arm's length between them and C.E., negotiating and communicating with Judith Wurm instead. As much as C.E. tried to stay in the loop, he believed that the bank and Judith worked hand-in-hand to keep him out of all decisions about the sale of C.E. Inc. to the detriment of his financial future.

One would think that, if the bank wasn't willing to sustain the company any longer, they would have jumped at pursuing the offer. Yet they ignored a possible sale and, in the process, left C.E out. The bank was calling all the shots. Why would they do this? Why would they take action to end their financial relationship with C.E.'s company and not help it until federal contract awards, which were just around the corner, came in to make C.E. Inc. into a profitable business?

Shortly after the receipt of the northeast's company's offer, the bank hired a team to manage the sale of the so-called 'distressed' company. Neither C.E. nor his management team had much to say about the bank's broker and other bank representatives, much less how they would execute the sale of the C.E. Inc.'s assets. Judith, as CFO, was the only company officer who played a significant role in working with the bank's representatives on the asset sale process.

Kane Hunter, the bank's vice president and his associate, Barry Liar, were the two main decision-makers assigned to represent the bank. They hired attorney Sean Sneek to represent the bank in the sale. He was not unknown to C.E. Inc.—Sean had also been commissioned by the bank when it took the old company, Zee Industries into and out of Chapter Eleven. During that period, the mild-mannered Sneek befriended C.E. and his management team as the new company started operations. I became acquainted with Sean over the many dinners that C.E. and I shared with him. Initially, it was Sean alone but we later met with his wife, a gregarious and lovely woman I came to like very much. Our dinners were pleasant occasions. Sean and his wife seemed honest and trustworthy. And Sean, especially, complimented C.E. at every turn about how he was running the company.

The other bank hire was Archer Knave from a company out of Minneapolis. But C.E. and his management team weren't aware of how Knave came to be hired to run the sale of C.E. Inc.'s assets. There were rumors that Knave may have done business in the past with Sneek and Hunter, or with Simon Green and Horace Steel, the eventual bidders of C.E.'s company's assets, or perhaps all of them.

C.E. had little choice but to cooperate with the bank's team: They ran the show. The bank's preferred stock gave them the muscle to do what they wanted, even against C.E. and his management team's wishes. The bank's main concern may have been to sell at a market value price previously determined at $30-35 million. That amount was included in a report done by Knave, commissioned by the bank. To do otherwise, the bank could be violating its fiduciary responsibility to the management team by forcing C.E. and his two officers to sell only the company's assets when the entire company was worth millions of dollars. Unfortunately, Sneek's back-and-forth between the bank and the management team led C.E. and Pancho to believe that Sneek was acting on their behalf. They realized later that they should have hired their own lawyer to watch their backs, but Sneek had persuaded them that he was seeking their best interests. He was active in discussions about all aspects of the asset sale deal, including everything from new contracts to the possibility of a board seat for C.E. with the newly-formed company, C.E. LLC, set up by Simon Green and Horace Steel. But to be actually placed on the board, C.E. was ordered by the bank to sign an incomplete framework of a draft contract sale agreement, which would precede a final agreement. Sneek verbally guaranteed that C.E. and the two other officers would be afforded the time to review and sign the agreement before the date of the asset sale, as specified by the bank. C.E. objected to signing a draft document, but Sneek advised him that the bank would sue him if he didn't comply. After C.E. signed the framework draft of the contract sale agreement—not the Final Sale Agreement, which was markedly different and had a different date—Sneek then announced he was not the management team's lawyer. Despite appearances and how he presented himself to C.E. and Pancho, he sternly reminded them both that, for the entire time of the asset sale, he had only represented the business entity and the bank.

C.E., Pancho, and Judith were kept in the loop by the bank during the early stages of the sale, though only Judith, as CFO, played an active part. All three understood that C.E. Inc. would be sold for approximately $34 million. The bank also told them that any potential buyer would be required to keep the management team in place for the sale to occur. That reason was as good as any for the management team to cooperate with the bank's sale decision. But somewhere along the way, that verbal 'retention of management' provision never materialized. That, along with a host of other issues related to their assured employment with the new company, C.E. LLC turned out to be lies by both the bank and the buyer that were detrimental to two of the three officers but helpful to the bank, the acquiring company, and Judith Wurm, its future employee.

In their attempts to learn about the process of seeking potential buyers for C.E. Inc., both C.E. and Pancho were troubled that Archer Knave had divulged very little to the management team about his criteria for identifying potential buyers. According to C.E. and Pancho, Knave arranged for the management team to meet with a couple of potential buyers, but they were not credible. Their offers in the $300,000 range were downright laughable at best and insulting at worst. Neither 'buyer' had an ounce of industrial type experience, they added. Which begs the question: why didn't Archer Knave pursue the northeast company that proposed to buy the entire company, not just its assets on behalf of its client? That company had deep pockets, revenues in the billions, had offered to keep the management team in place, and was on record as interested in buying all of C.E. Inc.

It soon became apparent to C.E. and Pancho that Knave's role in running the sale for the bank was nothing more than smoke and mirrors. He had produced zero credible potential buyers. They felt he was running a scam on them. It was their opinion that Knave knew who he wanted to take over C.E. Inc. In one of the meetings, Knave told C.E., O'Grady, and Wurm that a company in Rhode Island might want to buy the company. "And I can have them over here quickly to meet with you," he said.

A few days later, and much to C.E. and his two officers' surprise, Simon Green and Horace Steele, the principles of a minor and inconsequential private company, arrived to discuss the sale. The two men claimed their company had bought distressed companies in the past and flipped them successfully. But Knave did not provide credible information about the two men or the company's background to the company's management team. Several big questions lingered: What companies had these two guys' company bought and for how much? What was their success rate in flipping distressed companies? Who bought those companies, and how did their balance sheet and management teams fare after they were flipped? And should due diligence be done on this buying company by the bank through Archer Knave's firm or by some other process?

Simon Green and Horace Steele were touted by the bank and its business sale representatives, Sean Sneek and Archer Knave, as legitimate businessmen who had no agenda other than buying the company's assets and keeping the team together. But during their initial meeting, several things struck C.E. about the two strangers. *Who are these guys? Claiming all kinds of successful transactions that no one he knew had ever heard of.* In short, there was very little evidence of either their successes or their reputations.

Instead, C.E. focused on their military background as fellow veterans from their relatively short service stints. Green had served in the Air Force, while Steele had been in the Coast Guard. In Green's case, his military pedigree was particularly impressive on paper. He was a graduate of the Air Force Academy and his father was a retired Air Force colonel who had served heroically in the Korean war. C.E.'s trust in both fellows went up a notch based on that alone. As military men, C.E. felt a special kinship with them as part of the common creed most veterans hold dear: duty, honor, and country.

Regardless of anything C.E. said, I remained skeptical about Green and Steele's motives. If there was anything I remembered from catechism classes, it was the constant warning from the nuns and the priest that the devil walked among us. But I always expected him to stand out in a crowd. Sort of like the character depicted in movies and television: a tall white man dressed in black pants, a black shirt, wearing a black cape, sporting a short, pointed goatee complemented with a razor-thin mustache with tips slightly curled to match a sly grin, pitchfork in hand and points of white horns that adorned the top of a head with long slick-backed black hair. Green and Steele may not have looked like the devil, but they turned out to be the devil in disguise. In the end, I was right to be skeptical.

Shortly after their first meeting, Green's and Steele's company—who would form a new entity, C.E. LLC, for the acquisition of C.E.'s company's assets—presented a non-binding letter of intent to keep the management team intact. C.E. and his team expressed a sigh of relief. They would stay employed in the same positions, just as Sneek had said. Yet, C.E. and his team remained doubtful about Green and Steele, and I wasn't helping matters, constantly reminding both C.E. and Pancho that a non-binding document meant diddly-squat and warned them to watch their backs. They refused to listen because they believed Green and Steele were men of their word, that they would keep them employed, and pay them their due. But C.E. became conflicted. He wanted to believe they were men of their word, yet he was suspicious of them because there was very little information about them personally or their business successes, but C.E. felt he was running out of options to earn a living based on the bank's decision to sell C.E. Inc. and its ever-present lawsuit threats.

After C.E. and Pancho gave an extensive briefing on the company's current state and future contracts, Green, a massively overweight man, excitedly blurted: "We've gotta have this." All the while, his sweaty face seemed eager to take over a company with the potential to yield benefits beyond his wildest dreams. His much younger partner, Steele, stood by quietly, with an almost maniacal expression on his pimpled crater-laced face. His disturbing expression didn't go unnoticed by most in the room. "A creepy looking fellow, almost demonic," C.E. said when he came home that evening.

Green and Steele immediately sent a small team to conduct due diligence on C.E.'s company. They came the over the course of several days to examine the company's financial data and other relevant accounting information. They maintained a presence in the company's conference room that lasted until the purported purchase of the company's assets was completed about 90 days later.

When I learned from C.E. about Green and Steele's inordinate length of stay at the company's plant to conduct so-called due diligence, I couldn't help myself: "Tell them to get the fuck out."

But C.E. replied: "They said they'd keep the management team more than once, and that means keeping you and me financially secure." As he approached to hug me, I pushed him away and shouted: "Bullshit! "No one takes that long to conduct due diligence on a supposedly distressed and failing company. They either think they've got you backed into a corner, nowhere else to go, or they're fucking with you. These men are strangers; you don't know them. Yes, they're former military officers, but there are military men, and then there are good military men. Simon Green and Horace Steele didn't wear the uniform that long."

I paused for breath, then continued. "Let me tell you one other thing. This bunch are likely taking a long time because they discovered the millions in pre-awards and bids and proposals that are outstanding. Since they are only purchasing the company's assets, I'll bet you they are trying to figure out how to take all those contracts without paying for them and without having to go through a recompete process, which is required by the federal agency in charge of the contracts. You and I both know they can't legally take over those contracts if they haven't been awarded on the day of the asset sale. I'll bet you there is someone in the company who is helping them figure out how to take those contracts in violation of federal acquisition regulations requirements. Just remember this, if they are successful, whoever emerges from C.E. Inc. to get an important leading role in C.E. LLC is the person who helped them figure how to do it while betraying you and your executive team. I may not know much about these people, but I sure as hell don't trust a single one of those sons of bitches. You better keep your eyes wide open before they gouge them out."

A few days before the asset sale, Sneek transitioned from the mild-mannered friend and bank representative into an obnoxious and malevolent enemy. He badgered and degraded

C.E. at every chance, blaming him for C.E. Inc's downfall. Downfall? The company had approximately $50 million in pre-awarded government contracts, $150 million in the pipeline over a five-year period and was valued at between $30-35 million. Those numbers had been confirmed by the bank's commissioned company report done by Archer Knave when he was hired by the bank to sell the entire company at first, then only its assets.

In one of his tirades, Sneek rudely reiterated to C.E. why the bank had decided it could no longer keep loaning money to C.E. Inc. He accused C.E. of mismanagement and leading the company into bankruptcy. He asserted that because the company was in such dire financial straits, the bank couldn't find buyers. Their last recourse was the company belonging to Simon Green and Horace Steele and what they offered was a way out.

In hindsight, it became apparent that C.E. had been gaslighted into believing that the bank had no choice but to sell C.E. Inc's assets rather than the entire company as a viable business. That gaslighting paid off for all those involved in the sale of C.E. Inc's assets. C.E. was the only one left out in the cold, with no severance and only scraps of his former income to last him less than six months.

C.E. was known as one of the most formidable E-ring generals during his stint in the Pentagon. Yet, against the forces behind C.E. Inc's asset sale, he gave up the high ground and the battle. But any person beaten down long enough and without others to support him can believe himself to be a failure. I've learned that evil minds often rationalize their actions—and divert attention and focus—by blaming their victims.

Remember the initial sale inquiry C.E. received from the company in the northeast? A similar offer came from yet another interested buyer. A company based in Georgia that had previously partnered on a number of projects with C.E. Inc. showed a preliminary interest in purchasing the entire company. The bid was higher than that of C.E. LLC but once again the bank and its representatives found a way to ignore this offer.

A few hours after receipt of the letter from the second bidder, Archer Knave, along with Sean Sneek and Horace Steele, the very man conducting due diligence on C.E. Inc. and the eventual buyer of the company's assets, suppressed the tentative offer before it could lead to something formal. Archer Knave took quick action by reporting to C.E., Pancho O'Grady, Judith Wurm, and Sean Sneek that the date had expired for them to accept other bids so there was no need to meet with the Georgia-based company. By doing this, Knave closed all solicitations for bidders, leaving C.E. LLC the lone bidder and eventual owner of C.E. Inc.'s assets, even though their bid offer was lower than that made by the company in Georgia.

Around this time, the founder and chairman of the board of a large publicly traded company along with the company's president and CEO, met with C.E. and Pancho O'Grady. While the Midwest company had done some minor work with C.E. Inc., the executive officers weren't in the picture. They surprised C.E. when they suddenly showed up a day early from a previously scheduled meeting. The men were dressed in proper business attire but seemed anxious and rushed. Their conversation centered on one particular project they wanted to work on with C.E. Inc., but no deals were made that day. At the end of their meeting, C.E. mentioned that C.E. Inc. was being sold by its lender for approximately $34 million and asked if they were interested. But neither of the men responded to the question, rushing towards the building's front door to their waiting limousine. C.E. and Pancho's impression was that they were casing the plant instead of wanting to work with them. Little did they know at the time that both men would be connected to a future acquisition of C.E. Inc.'s key production line. And that part of the sale deal included a questionably-acquired federal proprietary number that belonged to C.E. Inc. That number was attached to the millions in pending contracts that C.E. Inc. had won under C.E.'s leadership.

After the Midwest company executives' visit, C.E. received an odd call from Charlie Kaka, a former board colleague from Zee Industries Inc. Kaka invited C.E. to meet him for lunch at a nearby private dining club. According to C.E., Kaka appeared fidgety and his face dripped in sweat as if he'd been running a marathon. Even his right hand, when C.E. shook it, was slimy and sticky like the back of a diseased old frog, prompting C.E. to quickly pull away. Before C.E. had a chance to even sit down on the hardwood Windsor style chair, Kaka blurted out his question. He wanted to know if C.E. had heard of a particular fellow from New Jersey who had built a national reputation for buying distressed companies, then flipping them for large profits? "The man is dead, but he sure left quite a legacy," Kaka said.

"What does that have to do with the company I am running?" C.E. asked.

"Well," Charlie answered, "the company that man built also lends money to distressed companies. If you ever want to get out from under your lender, that type of company may be what you're looking for. In fact, a couple of guys I know work in the same type of business over in Rhode Island. Have you heard of Simon Green and Horace Steele?"

C.E. said that he had never heard of the two men nor the business flipper from New Jersey —he hadn't at that time—and thought no more of it.

When the meeting was over, C.E. was concerned that someone had alerted Kaka that the company was having problems with the bank providing working capital. The money always came but not promptly, which added significant costs and losses to their operation. Only he, Judith Wurm, and Pancho O'Grady knew that, and he knew O'Grady didn't speak with Kaka. But Judith was another matter. C.E. told me in passing that he was aware of Judith's constant contact with Kaka before and during the asset sale but initially thought nothing of it. That is, until he concluded that Judith likely worked hand-in-hand with Charlie Kaka to help Kane Hunter, Simon Green, and Horace Steele push the company into a fire sale.

C.E. wasn't surprised that Judith and Charlie Kaka stayed in communication. They knew each other from Zee Industries Inc.'s days, and both resided in the same neighborhood. But C.E. complained to me more than once that he was concerned by how frequently Judith approached him to keep Kaka in the company's loop so he could help them to identify business prospects. C.E. chose to ignore Judith's pleas much to the anger of Judith. Kaka was not trusted by C.E. or by his COO Pancho O'Grady. They both believed that Kaka would kill to join C.E. Inc. in some capacity, only to do the company more harm than good. He had nothing to offer, just a lot of BS, according to both C.E. and Pancho.

During the many discussions of the company's asset sale, C.E. was left out of all decisions. He was copied on the email correspondence between the new buyers and the bank's representatives. But each time C.E. attempted to insert himself in the sale process, he was ignored by all those involved in the sale, including Judith, the person he had promoted to become the company's CFO. Judith never once warned C.E. about the potential land mines to look out for during the initial sale discussions, which became numerous. Instead, she insisted he had nothing to worry about. But she made the strong point to him more than once that he had no choice but to agree to sell the company's assets. This was her ongoing contribution to gaslighting C.E.

During the course of the asset sale, Judith's questionable loyalty revealed itself more than once. During one heated discussion, C.E. and Pancho asked Judith to join them in applying for a loan from another lender to pay off the company's debt balance to the bank so they could take over the company in a management buyout. Judith quickly rejected the idea. She sternly told C.E. and Pancho that the officers were not eligible to buy the company according to the contract between the company and the bank. Instead of asking Judith to point them to the clause in the contract that would substantiate her statement, they took her word for it.

C.E. should have pressed Judith to show him and Pancho the specific contract language, and if she could not, he had every reason to keep her from negotiating on behalf of the company or outright fire her. But at that point, C.E. felt he was becoming more irrelevant by the day. He was beginning to feel defeated by the ever-present circle of professional deceivers led by the bank. They criticized him as a lousy manager to serve their purpose. He became incredibly disappointed that his once-trusted CFO was part of the group that he felt was out to destroy him and his family's future. Especially galling to C.E. was Judith's complete disregard for all he had done to grow the company while advancing the rights and improve the working conditions of the company's employees, which included her.

It was not evident at the beginning, but towards the end of the asset sale discussions, it became crystal clear to C.E. that Judith was captured by the buyers of the company's assets and its seller.

"I can't blame her," C.E. said in a somber mood. "She thinks she is going to be a permanent part of C.E. LLC, while I can no longer do anything for her."

Judith may have had other reasons to see C.E. go down. She took umbrage whenever C.E. asked her to get to know the company's line workers who were mostly young men and women born in foreign countries. He often suggested she share lunch with them or make similar efforts to connect with them. C.E. made time for all his workers, regardless of their income level, or ethnic/racial background, and expected his senior staff to do the same. But, according to C.E. and Pancho, Judith seemed to have an aversion to mixing with the line workers and minorities. Also, Judith intensely disliked Pancho and never missed an opportunity to urge C.E. to fire him. But, much to her chagrin, C.E. liked and trusted Pancho. They had formed a close relationship many years earlier that no one could break, least of all Judith. That trust between C.E. and Pancho was to be compromised by the very same people who captured Judith, but more on this later.

I feel that things might have turned out differently for the company and for C.E. had the three officers worked closely together throughout the company's asset sale, especially during the final days. Judith's role was a vital one during the sale and after. But she made the choice to become a part of the devil's workshop set up by Green and Steele that would help to destroy her mentor's professional and financial life.

Once captured, Judith went all out to help Green and Steele obtain all of C.E. Inc., even at the risk of violating federal laws. She was all in. The day after C.E. Inc.'s asset sale took place, Judith ordered the production manager and her team to backdate federally-awarded product shipments amounting to almost a million dollars. Those monies should have been credited to Green and Steele's new company, C.E. LLC, because they were the new owners of C.E.'s company's assets. The date/time of sale is crucial as it is at that specific point that the sale of those products is considered revenue by the EPICOR System, the official U.S. Government accounting system. Instead, the federal government payments were made to C.E. Inc., a supposedly defunct entity. Wurm's order to backdate the shipments was not in keeping with the EPICOR System's federal rules and regulations and Judith most likely knew this. Yet, according to the production manager when she warned Judith that she was ordering them to commit a fraudulent act, her face turned beet-red, and she shouted: "You do what I say!" By forcing the staff to manipulate the shipping dates back to C.E. Inc., Judith forced the staff to commit a fraudulent act. But she didn't stop there. She also acted illegally by putting money back into C.E. Inc., which was a non-operating entity since its assets had been sold by the bank to C.E. LLC, the company belonging to Simon Green and Horace Steele. Every person involved in the asset sale knew that C.E. Inc. wasn't going to exist after its asset sale. At least that's what they told C.E. prior to the asset sale. Those words were echoed more than once by Sneek to C.E. and his two officers. "You don't have to worry about the company, it will cease to exist after the day of the sale." But that didn't happen. C.E. Inc. was kept alive by C.E. LLC, which they had no right to do since they didn't buy the entity, only its assets. Keeping C.E. Inc. alive allowed the board members of C.E. LLC to funnel money into its bank account from the shipping awards and possibly other sources as well, and unlawfully take its proprietary federal

31

number to benefit from its millions in federal contracts and discarding the entity after it was no longer of use to them

The shipments/federal award monies that Judith moved back to C.E. Inc. should have gone to C.E. LLC instead and recorded in the government's EPICOR system accordingly. They were, after all, the new owners of C.E. Inc.'s assets, and the shipment awards were assets. However, it was not possible to send those shipment awards to C.E. LLC because it didn't have a federally -assigned proprietary number at the time of the asset sale that allowed the new entity to legally accept the award money, or any other pending contract money for that matter. It's a standard and required rule that any new company planning to do business with the federal government must apply for its own assigned federal proprietary number. Once issued, the proprietary number becomes that company's identification number and belongs only to the entity that applied for it, and no other company can legally use it. The federally-assigned proprietary number can be transferred to another company, but only if the bidding company buys the entire company, not just its assets. Green and Steele should have applied for such a number before purchasing C.E.'s company's assets. They didn't do it then or after the asset sale. Instead, they took the proprietary number that belonged to C.E. Inc., an entity they did not purchase. It is my opinion that Judith Wurm, along with the officers of C.E. LLC, devised a scheme to keep those monies safe until C.E. LLC could figure a way to take them and spend them.

Judith was fully aware that the sale of C.E. Inc. was only for its assets only and not the entire company. She was one of the signatories on the contract sale agreement framework document and on the official state sale documents, which recorded that the assets had been sold. Although she signed the state documents, there were two other signatures on the same document that belonged to C.E., except he didn't sign them. Someone forged his signatures, which were then presented to the state as officially signed documents. Even though Judith signed and recorded documents with the state on the asset sale, there is no record with the state's tax office that C.E. LLC paid state taxes on the asset sale, which means they likely didn't pay federal taxes either.

Back to the federal monies that Judith manipulated. What happened to the funds received for those shipments? Did they end up in the bank account of C.E. Inc., or of C.E. LLC, or both? If those funds ended up in the account of C.E. LLC, what did the company officers do with those funds? Consider this: someone wired about $400,000 over several days after the asset sale toward the balance of C.E.'s Inc.'s old loan with the bank. Was the money wired from C.E. Inc.'s bank account, or was it wired from C.E. LLC's account? If the funds were wired from C.E. Inc.'s bank account, it means that C.E. LLC manipulated a process whereby C.E. Inc. paid into its old bank loan while C.E. LLC paid zero for the company's assets. If C.E. LLC did the actual wiring of $400,000 as payment to C.E. Inc.'s old bank loan, that was not part of the Final Contract Sale Agreement. Plus, that would change the terms of the asset sale, which had to be done with the approval of C.E. Inc.'s officers, namely, C.E. Levine, Pancho O'Grady, and Judith Wurm.

Why would Judith do all of this? Was it to stay in good graces with the new asset buyers, to remain on their payroll? Or was it to deceive the government into believing that C.E. Inc. continued to exist and had money to sustain itself until the $50 million or so in pending contracts—held up by the sequestration— were finally awarded? Or was it because C.E. LLC did not have a government-assigned proprietary number of its own to legally obtain the contract monies? As events unfolded and came to light, perhaps all these apply.

Years after the asset sale, I discovered that the bank had unilaterally decided to allow C.E. LLC to pay into C.E. Inc.'s old bank loan. The bank's decision changed the initial terms of the asset sale agreement between C.E. Inc. and C.E. LLC. Why would the bank allow this change without consulting with the three officers of C.E. Inc.? None of the three officers resigned from C.E. Inc., during and after its assets were sold. Technically speaking, they continued to be officers years after the asset sale. My sense is that the bank would have had to make them the same offer since they had the Right of First Refusal.

In its effort to put the asset sale of his company squarely on C.E.'s back, the bank required that the sale of C.E. Inc.'s assets be signed and executed by him as its company's president and CEO. The bank representatives made clear to C.E. and his management team that C.E. was responsible for selling the company's assets by being the officer in charge of the company. C.E. verbally rejected the order outright. Why should he sign when during the process of the sale when he had been left out of all decision making? He had always disagreed with the asset sale and its ridiculously lowball price offered by C.E. LLC. When C.E. resisted, Sean Sneek warned him that he had to sign the contract sale agreement framework document or the bank would sue him for failure to meet fiduciary responsibility.

One can understand that, if a company missed several of its required payments to its lender, had zero revenue, and had no potential to earn revenue, the lender would want to sell it any way it could. But that wasn't the case with C.E. Inc. Before his company's assets were sold, C.E. informed Kane Hunter that C.E. Inc. had pending federal contracts of approximately $50 million with a pipeline of $150 million-plus over a five-year cycle. He also stressed that federal contract money would start flowing into the company once sequestration ended, including a contract worth about $30 million over five years. Instead of wanting to learn more, Hunter, a Senior Vice President with the bank, pressed on with the asset sale. Sure enough, the $30 million-dollar contract was awarded by the government to C.E. Inc. six months after the asset sale. Yet, somehow, C.E. LLC, which had not submitted the original proposal to the federal government, ended up with the contract only a few weeks after it was awarded to C.E. Inc.

Banks have many rights, some not so friendly to the average consumer. That is why some elected officials have become a constant voice in the regulation of banks. In this case, the bank may have been exercising its right to do all that it did with C.E. Inc.'s asset sale, but to what end? Banks typically have one agenda: making money for their officers and investors by protecting and increasing their profit. They have an army of lawyers and lobbyists that defend their interests. Any small or moderate-sized company or individual that stands up to a bank will probably not succeed. Yet banks are a necessary evil. Society at large cannot survive without the existence of banks. After all, they are the institutions that supposedly keep our money safe and lend us money to buy everything from clothing and transportation to our homes. Like them or not, banks are a means to our financial survival and well-being. But they are often cruel and deceptive institutions. Their bottom line is to protect and increase their profit.

As in the case of C.E. Inc., if the bank claimed to suffer a loss on a federally-backed loan, it may be able to recoup its losses from the federal government. So, the sale of C.E. Inc. for much less than it was worth may not have ended so badly for the bank as it did for us and others.

When Kane Hunter first approached C.E. to find a buyer for C.E. Inc. for $34 million, the management team was not unhappy. C.E. knew the worth of the federal contracts on the horizon. The millions in contracts would stabilize the company, which would then be poised to earn a profit for the bank. Surely, they would see the value of its long-term future. But he was dead wrong. A bank can make money by losing money. The bank made the clear choice to put one company out of business and bring in a newly-formed company that walked away with the other company's millions worth of federal contracts through a federally assigned proprietary number they did not rightfully own and did not pay for its full value.

For months, Kane Hunter told C.E. and his management team that the bank was selling C.E. Inc. for approximately $34 million. Yet the bank sprang their decision to a surprised C.E. to sell only the assets for $3.4 million two weeks before the scheduled sale date. C.E. struggled for days about signing the contract sale agreement framework document that had been put in front of him by the bank and by its representative, Sean Sneek. They brought more pressure to bear on him. Remember, at the beginning of C.E. Inc.'s formation, C.E. gave his two key officers each 33 percent of the shares. They exercised their power and urged C.E. to sign, or else they would vote against him. Both Pancho and Judith stressed to C.E that they could not lose their jobs. Unknown to C.E. at the time, they were both offered employment contracts by Green and Steele. But Pancho and Judith didn't last long in the new company. Pancho was let go six weeks after the asset sale, while Wurm left after a year. I suspect that Judith walked away with a wallet much fatter than Pancho's and certainly fatter than C.E.'s.

Like a faithful soldier, Pancho remained in the foxhole with C.E. until a few days before the sale, when he took a call from

Simon Green. In their brief conversation, Simon asked Pancho to join the new company, which he accepted without a moment of hesitation. The hook was in. Pancho's decision served to split up the management team—to the detriment of C.E. Judith was already on their side, so all Green and Steele, along with Kaka, needed was co-opt Pancho, which was easily done. C.E. was outnumbered and outmaneuvered. He had no choice but to sign the contract sale agreement framework document that had been dangled before him for days. Or was he out of options?

C.E. had leverage. He could have told the bank and Green, Steele and Kaka that all pending contracts that had been won by C.E. Inc. could not be counted as assets because they had not been fully awarded. Federal law (41 U.S.C. § 15, the 'Anti-Assignment Act') prohibits the transfer of government contracts to a third party, but it also allows the government to make exceptions to the rule if the parties go through a process of 'novation' for the acquirer to become the new contractor. And C.E. could have demanded that if Green and Steele wanted those contracts, they would have to legally novate them with the assistance of C.E. Inc. and be required to pay for their actual value, which was a lot more than their $3.4 bid. And, while at it, he could have pointedly asked Green, Steele and Kaka if their newly-formed company, C.E. LLC, had been assigned its own proprietary number. If they answered no, C.E. could have told them to get the fuck out of his office and not return unless they had the number, otherwise he was going to report them to the bank's representatives, and everyone connected with the asset sale and terminate the sale. And in that case, the bank wouldn't have a leg to stand on to pursue filing a lawsuit against C.E. Except C.E. didn't press them on this issue because he believed that C.E. LLC had applied for its own federal proprietary number, since he knew they were required by federal acquisition regulations to do so.

The decision to have C.E. Inc. subcontract its contract winnings with C.E. LLC was a viable option. It was an idea first floated by Green and Steele and highly welcomed by C.E. since it was a win-win for both companies. C.E. Inc. would continue to exist under C.E.'s leadership as president and CEO. C.E. would control the contracts that he and Pancho O'Grady had worked so hard to win while slowly transferring that work to C.E. LLC. But, to adhere to the required process, C.E. LLC would have to pay the full the value of the contracts and would have to present its proprietary number and demonstrate that it had the capital to sustain those multi-million-dollar contracts. The process would allow C.E. LLC to be in a position to eventually legally obtain all of C.E. Inc.'s contracts and win future contracts on their own merit. C.E. could then ease out of the company, making it a fair transaction for all the parties. But here again, the problem facing C.E. LLC was that the company didn't have a federally-assigned proprietary number of its own to legally novate or subcontract either current or pending contracts that belonged to C.E.'s company and didn't seem to have the capital to pay for the contracts' full value. Had the bank allowed C.E. to hold these discussions with C.E. LLC's officers, he would have blown their proprietary number and money issues cover, and their scheme to take over all of C.E. Inc. and to throw him overboard would have failed. But the bank kept C.E. from getting involved in the asset sale process from the outset. Who knows how things might have turned out for C.E. Inc., for C.E. himself, and for all other company employees?

C.E. had other options. Since he disagreed to sell C.E. Inc.'s assets for so little money and since his two management team members didn't support his decision, he could have sued them for allowing the assets to be sold for such an undervalued figure. Or he could have submitted his resignation to Pancho and Judith. By doing that, he would have separated himself from his company, and the bank would have had to pay him the remaining two years of severance as stated in his employment contract, which amounted to almost $1.3 million. In fairness, C.E. discussed his desire to resign with Sean Sneek. But Sneek rebuffed him, telling him he didn't need to bother with C.E. Inc. because it was going to be dissolved immediately after the asset sale and, in any case, C.E., would become a well-compensated board member of C.E. LLC and a decision-maker of all things to come within the new company.

The agreed-upon payment between C.E. LLC and the bank for C.E. Inc.'s assets was another concern of C.E.'s. He understood that in his role as president and CEO of C.E. Inc., C.E. LLC was going to pay him $3.4M so that he would in turn pay the bank. But he did not receive the payment. Years later that concern was compounded when he learned that C.E. Inc. had processed official state sale documents with his signature on it which he didn't sign and which stated that the buyer (C.E. LLC) would pay in cash or in the manner so dictated by the seller (C.E., on behalf of C.E. Inc.) $3.4 million for C.E. Inc.'s assets. The document implied that C.E. would take that money and pay the bank. But here again, C.E. never received payment on behalf of his company from C.E. LLC before or after the asset sale.

This prompted C.E. to question the bank about who paid the $3.4 million as stated in the official state sale document. At first the bank ignored C.E.'s request but eventually provided documentation regarding the sale transactions of C.E. Inc.'s assets to C.E. LLC. The bank's documents revealed several bank wire transactions of $3 million. The originating source was some LLC finance group (the transaction was coded as a customer transfer) located in the mid-Atlantic region. That LLC finance group then sent the money to a bank located in another state and that bank moved the money to the bank that was the lender of C.E.'s company and that bank then moved the money yet again to the lending bank's headquarters. But the documentation presented by the bank did not show that C.E. LLC was the one responsible for the money transfers.

One thing is for certain—C.E. LLC failed to pay the $3.4 million to C.E. as specified in the official state sale document, and they didn't pay state sale taxes on their asset purchase. Adding to the confusion, the document provided by the lending bank showed someone wired $3 million to the bank's office headquarters into C.E. Inc.'s old loan with the bank. This happened a day after the official asset sale. It begs the question: how could two different transfers of $3 million be made to the bank, one to the bank's regional office one day, and the other to C.E. Inc.'s bank loan debt the following day, with no acknowledgment of who wired those monies? Was it the same $3 million initially wired from the LLC finance group? And who was the originator of the money wired?

If you are up to your ass in confusion, read on! Over the course of a week, someone wired close to $400,000.00 into C.E. Inc.'s loan debt with the bank. Again, the records don't show who wired those monies. Was the money sent from C.E. Inc.'s bank account and, if so, who did it since the company was not supposed to be operational? Or was it wired from C.E. LLC's bank account? If it was from C.E. Inc.'s bank account, then C.E. Inc. paid into its old loan while C.E. LLC paid zero for their purchase of C.E. Inc.'s assets. If the money was wired was from C.E. LLC that was not part of the Final Sale Contract Agreement. C.E. LLC did not buy C.E. Inc.'s stock as an operating entity. The transaction was an asset sale, and as stated in the Final Sale Contract Agreement, C.E. LLC was not assuming C.E. Inc.'s debt.

Why was the money used to make payment on a bank loan owed by C.E. Inc. moved around so much? Who wired the $3 million, including the additional $400,000? If it was one of the principals from C.E. LLC, where did they get the money? Why would they assume and pay off part of a debt that was not their responsibility as per the Final Sale Contract Agreement? Could it have been that some of C.E. Inc.'s $50M in new contracts were awarded and began producing, and C.E. LLC used C.E. Inc.'s account funds to pay toward its very old bank loan? Or did C.E. LLC pay into C.E. Inc.'s loan using the funds from the backdating shipment scheme carried out by Judith Wurm? Or did C.E. LLC take the contract monies awarded under C.E.'s leadership by siphoning them into their company's bank account and then use them to pay off some of C.E. Inc.'s bank loan? Either way, it appears that C.E. LLC paid zero for C.E. Inc.'s assets. If that were the case, why would the bank allow C.E. LLC to do this? Here again, the argument is not whether a bank can do what they did and allow C.E. LLC to do what they did. Banks have many privileges, and they exercise them daily. The message here is to be careful in dealing with banks. They'll upend your life in a moment's notice and won't give their decision and your loss a second thought.

Another concern of C.E.'s was: Why did the bank take only $3.4 million and, apparently, forgive the remaining $3 million of the debt owed by C.E. Inc.? Why wouldn't the bank give C.E. and his two officers that deal? Or why wouldn't the bank instead give C.E., Pancho, and Judith an opportunity to buy all of C.E. Inc. and pay off all its debt owed to the bank? Especially since the management team had the Right of First Refusal for any transaction regarding the sale of the company. By not giving them this opportunity, the bank cheated its common shareholders, while providing C.E. LLC an open path to acquire all of C.E. Inc.'s current and pending contracts worth millions. C.E. LLC would have had to pay a hell of a lot more money to acquire all the contracts than the paltry amount of $3.4 million dollar scheme they cooked up with the bank for C.E. Inc.'s assets. Yet C.E. LLC ended up with all of C.E. Inc.'s pending and future contracts for pennies on the dollar, or even nothing.

For years, C.E. kept trying to the get to the bottom of all that went down between his former company and the bank. At one point, he communicated with a federal agency that oversees sale and company losses reported by banks. In one of the communiques from the bank to the federal agency, the bank denied they sold C.E. Inc.'s assets, stating they were only the lender. But in correspondence from lawyers involved in the asset sale, they acknowledged the bank was the seller of C.E. Inc.'s assets. They were not a passive participant. The bank, through Kane Hunter and Barry Liar, actively drove the asset sale from start to finish. They threatened to sue C.E. for violating his fiduciary responsibility if he didn't sign the contract sale agreement framework document. Yet it appears that the bank broke its fiduciary responsibility to C.E. and his two officers, Pancho O'Grady and Judith Wurm, in several ways: by ordering them to sign a framework sale document that was not the final sale document, by selling the assets of a well-managed and profitably poised company for far less than its value, and by changing the terms of the asset contract sale agreement to allow C.E. LLC to pay into a part of C.E. Inc.'s loan with the bank without giving the same opportunity to its three officers. All these actions by the bank allowed C.E. LLC to end up with millions they did not earn, while foregoing paying both state and federal taxes on their acquisition of C.E. Inc.'s assets.

As the asset sale pressed on, C.E. felt he was becoming more irrelevant by the day. He was beginning to feel defeated by the ever-present circle of professionals led by the bank. They had criticized him as a lousy manager and blamed him for the bank having to sell C.E. Inc.'s assets. It was dawning on C.E. that he would not be able to stave off the bank's heavily-armed and armored solicitors. It was incredibly disappointing to learn that all he had done to grow the company into the millions, to advance the rights and improve the working conditions of the company's employees, interested no one and he was on his way out. His spirit was irrevocably broken into many pieces—he hasn't been the same person since the day the assets of C.E. Inc. were sold. Shortly after, his health began to fail.

This is likely not the first time the bank has been responsible for ending a well-run company with a bright and prosperous future. The bank literally gave away all of C.E. Inc., not just its assets, to C.E. LLC, but for what reason(s)?

C.E. didn't seek my advice when facing his most difficult career challenge. Instead, he thought he was protecting me by not sharing the details of how he lost his company. And that was a fight I would have happily joined in and fought at his side if he had only let me.

Thomas Jefferson's words are still as relevant today as when he said them back in the 1700s. They bear repeating: "I sincerely believe that banking establishments are more dangerous than standing armies and that the principle of spending money to be paid by posterity, under the name of funding, is but swindling futurity on a large scale." Amen to that!

Chapter **3**

Life can turn on a dime

"Truly evil people don't just hurt others. They take pride in the pain they cause and then try to blame their victims." —Susan Outwater

"General, we need you to be a part of the new company. You are of value in helping Gustavo Feo get started as the new president of C.E. LLC. You're the one with all the government contacts."

When Charlie Kaka spoke those words during a meeting just before C.E. Inc.'s asset sale closing, Horace Steele and Gustavo Feo nodded in agreement. During the meeting, Kaka pressed C.E. to sign on as a board member of the new company that would acquire C.E. Inc.'s assets.

Charlie Kaka was an obnoxious hulk of a man—gruff, mannerless, and lacking any positive qualities of character or charisma that could have made him a likeable or believable person. He had served on the board of Zee Industries Inc. along with C.E. when the company exited Chapter Eleven bankruptcy. They got along, but Kaka wasn't the type of fellow C.E. would have a drink with after work or any other time.

Yet, on a cold and dreary day, Kaka was brought on by Simon Green and Horace Steele to get C.E., his former board colleague, to sign the contract sale agreement framework document that C.E. wasn't keen on signing in exchange for a relatively low-paid consulting agreement and board seat with C.E. LLC that he was even less inclined to sign. Kaka locked eyes with C.E., telling him that if he signed the contract sale agreement framework document presented by the bank, they would appoint him as a consultant and a board member of their newly formed company, "You go from one company to another," and that's great for all of us," C.E. remembered Kaka telling him.

But Kaka wasn't brought in to be an honest broker. Instead, as a former board colleague, Simon Green and Horace Steele brought him in to help them deceive C.E. into signing an incomplete contract sale agreement framework document that likely had no legal standing, in exchange for a consulting agreement they intended to reduce and quickly terminate. That was quickly evident. The ink on C.E.'s signature had barely dried when C.E. LLC, through Kaka, reduced the value of the consulting agreement to practically nothing and then proceeded to have him kicked off C.E. LLC's board altogether. Charlie Kaka was Green and Steele's bitch. I've often wondered how that man can sleep at night. In my opinion, he went out of his way to hurt not just C.E. and our family but many of C.E. Inc.'s honest and hard-working employees—and this from a person that calls himself a Christian.

In retrospect, Kaka was jealous of C.E. when he was chosen as the CEO of a company he wished he had led. He lurked in the background for several years until he found a way to not only oust C.E. from the company and, in my opinion, worked aggressively to destroy him personally and professionally. He joined ranks with Simon Green and Horace Steele, even more evil and common men. All three of them treated C.E. in the most cruel and despicable manner I've ever witnessed in all my years of working in both the public and private sectors. They may be living high on the hog, but I am here to remind them that the money they acquired by selling C.E. Inc.'s contracts, weren't theirs to sell, to a third party.

While Kaka spoke, the room was as still as a winter night, but one that was filled with silent predators. A snake oil salesman would have been put to shame by Kaka that day. He was a huckster at the height of form, selling the board seat convincingly to C.E. as if God Almighty was his witness, lying through his crooked and yellow-stained teeth.

That evening, before C.E. signed either of the two documents, we had a tense and combative conversation right out of a *War of the Roses* movie scene. "You're not signing anything until you get a lawyer," I demanded.

"Bonita, you know more than anyone that I don't have the money needed to hire a lawyer," C.E. stressed. "We've made good money, but most of it was spent on the old company's stock, which we lost. Our income covers living expenses and that's about it."

As he walked out of the small kitchen in our townhome, I followed, climbing the narrow stairs closely behind him: "I don't trust a single one of those lying sons of bitches!" I screamed. "Get rid of them, before it's too late!"

But, being the quiet and thoughtful man he is known to be, C.E. ignored my words and said we'd finish the discussion the next day. I was as furious as I'd ever been with the man that had swept me off my feet almost 40 years earlier. Back then, and for most of those four decades, he could do no wrong. But on this day, I felt he was doing everything wrong and then some. The next day, I arranged for him to speak with a lawyer friend of mine, but C.E. refused, saying in an angry yet defeatist tone I had rarely—maybe never—heard from him: "What the fuck over, they've got the upper hand, Bonita."

"How in God's earth can you say that?" I protested, trying to get him to listen. "You don't have to sign anything! The bank doesn't have the grounds to sue you based on some cockamamie incomplete so-called contract sale agreement framework."

C.E. didn't want to hear any more. He started to walk away from the kitchen table, but I got up in his face: "If you sign the so-called contract sale agreement framework, you will allow the bank to get away with screwing you, Pancho, and Judith out of the millions of dollars you all rightfully earned. Especially you. You do realize that, don't you?" My words fell on deaf ears, but I persisted. "Not only that, by signing that incomplete contract sale agreement framework, you're allowing the bank to tell the world you agreed to sell your company's assets for a mere $3.4 million, when everyone knows that company is worth millions. There is no court in the land that will uphold such an incomplete document. So don't sign the fucking nothing document, nor the pathetic consultant contract offer from C.E. LLC."

I paused, but he said nothing so I continued my rant. "Listen to this, what if the other board members of C.E. LLC, Green, Steele, and Kaka, vote to let you go before the expiration date of the cockamamie consulting contract? Board memberships generally don't carry a protective clause. They could oust you from the board in a New York minute. Have you thought of that? Do you realize without your income, we stand to lose everything? And at this stage in either of our lives, who in the world will hire us to make up for the lost income?" C.E. stared at me without replying. I had never seen him so resigned and so passive. I kept on, "Let me ask you this, are these the type of men you'd feel safe sharing a foxhole with?"

That brought an unexpected and highly emotional response from C.E.: "Hell no!" His yell was so loud I was sure the entire neighborhood had heard him.

"Well, there you have it! Cut your ties with those lying sons of bitches, before it's too late," I urged.

C.E. shook his head. "The bank is running the show. They'll sue me if I don't sign the document."

"Fuck the bank and the horse it rode in on!" I shouted. "It sounds to me like the bank is taking the company from you and literally gifting it to C.E. LLC. I am wondering what's in it for Kane Hunter and Barry Liar and what I am wondering about those two I won't even repeat in your presence."

But they defeated C.E. without a fight. In the end, C.E. did as the bank ordered. Along with Pancho and Judith, he signed a document titled "Contract Sale Agreement Framework." It was nothing more than an outline for a future Final Contract Sale Agreement. The 17-page document comprised signature pages, boilerplate information, and a reference that C.E., as CEO of C.E. Inc. was selling its assets to C.E. LLC but it did not include the specifics found in a legally-binding asset sale document. The signing was a game changer. One that literally destroyed our financial lives from which we've barely been able to recover.

To be fair, during that fateful meeting with the officers of C.E. LLC and representatives of the bank, C.E. pressed the group and asked why he and the two officers were signing such a sketchy, non-specific document. Sean Sneek piped in and urged him to sign, then explained that the document was to get the asset sale ball rolling. He convincingly stated that C.E. and his two officers would get a copy of the Final Contract Sale Agreement at closing for their review, approval, and signature. "Don't worry," he said, too easily smoothing away C.E.'s concern, "it will not be much different from what you are about to sign. Besides, you will be on C.E. LLC's board of directors. What's not to like!"

C.E. did not receive and read the Final Contract Sale Agreement until four years after the asset sale. And that copy came to him from the bank's Barry Liar. When C.E. read the complete Final Contract Sale Agreement, he found many items that were never discussed by the bank's representatives or the buyers of C.E. Inc.'s assets nor included in the initial framework document. They were particularly damaging to C.E.'s livelihood and, indirectly, mine. One item, a non-compete clause—without the compensation seen in most mergers and acquisition transactions—stated that C.E. could not work in a similar industrial company for several years. Another noted that C.E. LLC owned the name of C.E. forever and that all of C.E. Inc.'s pending and future contracts were owned by C.E. LLC as part of the asset sale.

It's my opinion that this new document triggered the stress level that affected C.E.'s health even more. Even though the bank threatened a lawsuit to get C.E. to sign the basic contract sale agreement framework document, he stated more than once that he would never have agreed to such a restrictive final sale agreement. How could C.E. earn a living if he could not seek work in a company doing similar work as that of his former company? And it is insane to believe he would allow Green and Steele to name their new company the same as his for always. In doing so, C.E. LLC stood to misrepresent itself as the buyer of all of C.E. Inc., not just its assets, allowing them to claim that C.E. LLC and C.E. Inc. were one and the same company.

Green and Steele packed all they could into the final version of the Contract Sale Agreement that greatly benefited them personally and their new company, while literally destroying C.E.'s future and well-being. The document included language that all active and future contracts belonged to C.E. LLC and claimed that C.E. allowed them to own them by signing the Final Contract Sale Agreement. Except that C.E. didn't sign the final version document. But even more importantly, based on the federal acquisition regulations, C.E. did not have the legal authority to turn over all his company's current contracts, pending or otherwise, to C.E. LLC, especially since the company didn't have a federally-assigned proprietary number to receive those contracts. For C.E. LLC to legally obtain any and all contracts that C.E. Inc. had in hand at the time of the asset sale would have required C.E. LLC to either have them novated by C.E. as the president and CEO of C.E. Inc., or subcontract to C.E. Inc.

But regardless of whether C.E. LLC decided to novate or subcontract the contracts, the company was required to provide their own federally-assigned proprietary number to legally obtain those contracts. Instead of legitimately applying for its own federally-assigned number, C.E. LLC, a few weeks after the asset sale, found a way to convince the federal government to allow them to take the federally-assigned proprietary number that belonged to C.E.'s company, an entity they did not purchase as part of the asset sale, thus bypassing the required federal novation or subcontract requirements.

As far as all of C.E. Inc.'s pending and future contracts scheduled to be awarded after the asset sale, C.E. LLC was required per the federal acquisition regulations to notify the federal agencies that they were purchasing C.E. Inc.'s assets and that the entity known as C.E. Inc. would have a new name, Jet Inc., within ten days after the asset sale. They were the owners only of C.E.'s company's assets, not the entity, but it was their responsibility to inform the federal government of the sale details that included millions of contract dollars that had not yet been awarded at the time of the sale. The federal agencies in charge of the contracts would then be required to recompete all pending contracts won by C.E. Inc. under C.E.'s leadership. This is the government's way of ensuring that federal contracts were not being fulfilled by some indiscriminate company that did not participate in the bidding and proposal process. It's unfair to those who competed for the contract to learn that a company that did not participate in the competition—or did not have the contracts novated properly—ended up with the award. C.E. LLC would have had to submit a new proposal and compete with other companies for all C.E.'s company's pending contracts, especially the huge and essential pending $30 million contract.

Its's my opinion that the key reason the federal agencies did not recompete the contracts was because C.E. LLC showed up with C.E.'s Inc.'s proprietary number, misrepresenting to them that they were one and the same company.

This was a shell game that they won. C.E. LLC took over company worth millions that was deliberately labeled distressed by its bank lender/owner. The ploy of buying the so-called distressed company's assets for pennies on the dollar could even be illegal. In any other company sale, C.E. LLC would have had to pay the full value of the entity based on the millions of federal contract dollars that it had been awarded and pre-awarded per its federally-assigned proprietary number. But the bank decided to ignore C.E. Inc.'s full value, calling it instead a distressed company to justify their selling the company's assets for a mere $3.4M to a company with no industrial experience and one lacking the necessary requirements to meet basic federal acquisition regulations.

A key ingredient of the asset sale was the government contracts that C.E. Inc. had been awarded on the date of the asset sale which were minor in nature. But even those small budgeted contracts could not end in the hands of C.E. LLC unless C.E. Levine as president of the company that won those contracts novated them to the newly formed company and of course they would have had to possess a federally-assigned proprietary number for the government to allow them those contracts. As a matter of reference, Pancho and Judith who were once officers of C.E. Inc. could have possibly also novated the small contracts but were not eligible because they became permanent employees of C.E. LLC on the day of the asset sale.

The other bids and proposals—which were huge potential federal contracts for C.E. Inc. totaling about $50 million—had not been awarded at the time of sale. Based on federal acquisition regulations, they could not belong to C.E. LLC, regardless of language found in the final version of the Contract Sale Agreement. It would have been illegal for C.E. to novate them as part of the asset sale since they hadn't been awarded at the time. The only way those millions of dollars' worth of contracts could have legally gone to C.E. LLC was if they had subcontracted with C.E.'s company, and of course, if they had a federally-assigned proprietary number to go with it.

Further, for C.E. LLC to legally acquire C.E. Inc.'s current and pending contracts, the new company president, Gustavo Feo, was required to sign the novation on behalf of C.E. LLC, or arrange to subcontract with C.E Inc. And, as president of C.E. LLC, it was also Feo's responsibility to show proof that C.E. LLC had applied for and received its required federally-assigned proprietary number to legally obtain the contracts through either process. But he made the choice to ignore the legal route.

C.E. LLC came to the asset purchase room without its own federally-assigned proprietary number in order to legally obtain C.E. Inc.'s existing and pending contracts. And it seemed they had little or no money to pay for C.E.'s company's assets, never mind paying full value for all of C.E. Inc.'s pending contracts worth millions of dollars. But with the help from the bank, C.E. LLC ended up with millions worth of federal contracts that didn't belong to their company, and which they turned around and resold, making them rich beyond their dreams.

The C.E. LLC leadership was aware their company had to have C.E. Inc. novate its contracts to them. Horace Steele specifically directed to keep C.E. Inc. active so that its officers would help novate the pending contracts. Was this a naïve or purposeful directive by Steele? Did he know that none of the officers could novate any contracts to his new company that hadn't been awarded at the asset sale date? A federal contract must be fully awarded to novate or subcontract them to the purchasing entity. And the purchasing entity must possess its own federal proprietary number for the contract process to legally take place. To confuse matters worse, the wording in the final version of the Contract Sale Agreement stated that C.E.'s company would change its name ten days after the sale of C.E.'s company's assets, but it didn't state who was to make that name change and it didn't happen. How could Steele expect C.E. Inc. to novate its contracts to the Green and Steele company ten days before its name was to change? Anyone who has done business with the federal government knows it doesn't work that fast. And wouldn't this name change confuse the government agencies that pre-awarded contracts to C.E. Inc.? In the end, neither Horace Steele nor anyone associated with his company called upon C.E. to help novate C.E. Inc.'s current or pending contracts or to change his former company's name.

This raises the question: Why didn't Steele reach out to C.E. to novate or subcontract those contracts? Could it have been because he didn't need C.E. Inc. to novate or subcontract once his company had taken C.E. Inc.'s federally-assigned proprietary number only a few weeks after the asset sale?

C.E. LLC took a highly questionable and risky shortcut by appropriating the proprietary number that legally belonged to C.E. Inc., an entity they did not purchase, adding the number to their company's profile through the federal government's System for Award Management (SAM). This can only be conveyed through a stock sale, not an asset sale. By seizing C.E. Inc.'s federally-assigned number, C.E. LLC ended up with all of C.E.'s company's millions worth of pending contracts that had not been awarded at the time of the asset sale, and for which they paid zero dollars.

C.E. LLC, which did not submit the original $30 million proposal to the federal government, ended up with the contract. How was it that they ended up with the contract that was pre-awarded to C.E. Inc.? Did the federal agency that awarded the contract think that C.E. LLC and C.E. Inc. were the same company because they had the same proprietary number and similar name? The contract specialist, Jonathan Taken, representing the federal agency, could have investigated further. But it appears that he chose not to thoroughly review how C.E. LLC ended up with the proprietary number of an entity they didn't purchase, because the involved parties were either inept or part of the scheme.

Transferring a federally-assigned proprietary number from one company to another is highly complicated and arduous. Yet, Carol Nothing, a former employee of C.E. Inc. who was kept on by the C.E. LLC managed to complete this difficult task, bragged that she had defeated the system. What exactly did Ms. Nothing tell the SAM staff for them to approve the transfer of C.E. Inc.'s proprietary number to C.E. LLC?

In his further review of all things that transpired after the asset sale, C.E. was befuddled to learn that the bank allowed C.E. LLC to pay only part of C.E. Inc.'s loan balance. But the real stake in his heart was discovering that C.E. LLC's lawyers submitted a copy of the Final Contract Sale Agreement to the Court in response to C.E.'s lawsuit against C.E. LLC. This was a document he did not review, approve, and sign. And, to further raise the level of his anger and frustration, he discovered that the pages with C.E.'s and Gustavo Feo's signatures and the signature page of the three officers were taken from the contract sale agreement framework document, reproduced and inserted into the Final Contract Sale Agreement. In doing this, C.E. LLC's legal team introduced a fraudulent document to the court. Were they aware the document they presented to the court was never reviewed, approved, and signed by C.E. and his two officers? Were they even aware that the contract sale agreement framework document with a different date from the final version of the Contract Sale Agreement existed?

Unfortunately, C.E. and his management team didn't have legal counsel representing their interests in the sale. They felt they didn't need one because Sean Sneek led them to believe he was looking out for their interests throughout the sale process by advising and explaining what their role would be with C.E. LLC. Sean's ethical duty from day one should have been to lay out the legal groundwork for the management team. He should have explained that he wasn't their personal lawyer and urged them to hire their own lawyer to protect their interests in the sale. Only after the three officers at his urging signed a framework of a document that had no legal force did he advise them that he represented C.E.'s company on behalf of the bank and never represented them.

After C.E. signed the contract sale agreement framework document, Sneek and Kaka ordered him to leave the company's premises and not to return. "He wasn't needed," they said. The once highly beloved and respected head of his company, in a snap of a finger, was out on his ear with nothing but his faith and instinct for self-preservation. It was like skinning him alive. But C.E. had every reason to return to his old company's headquarters. He was invited to be on the board of C.E. LLC and his presence would be required since Horace Steele specifically said that he wanted to keep C.E. Inc. alive so its officers would novate its contracts to C.E. LLC. That turned out to be a lie. In my opinion, Sneek and Kaka were in on the conspiracy with Green and Steele to take all of C.E. Inc.'s pending and pre-awarded contracts without following federal novation laws and without paying the full value of the contracts, which was in the high millions. The company's board offer was cooked up to get C.E. to sign an incomplete so-called contract agreement document and then toss him overboard. Sneek and Kaka likely also knew that Green and Steele never intended to novate or subcontract the contracts since C.E. LLC had developed a scheme to get them without following federal acquisition regulations.

In their efforts to continue swaying and confusing C.E. and implying to the world that he had signed the Final Contract Sale Agreement, Kaka, who was now the chairman of C.E. LLC's board of directors, convened a meeting of the new company's board on the day of the asset sale. It wasn't a real meeting, but rather a ruse to get C.E. to think he was part of the new board. C.E.'s only role that day was to sign that he acknowledged and accepted a seat on the board of C.E. LLC. Charlie called C.E. to tell him that the signing by all board members would be done remotely since he knew C.E. was busy and lived far away. C.E. dismissed Charlie's excuse and offered to drive to his former office and sign the document so he could review it in its entirety but was quickly rebuffed by Kaka. Instead, C.E. received a blank signature page by courier that Kaka asked to be signed but not dated. C.E., went against his better judgment and signed the blank page while the courier waited for him to do so. He felt he had no other choice; it was sign or you are off the board type of feeling. He came to regret that decision. The three other board members, Charlie Kaka, Simon Green, and Horace Steele signed another undated page version. The two separate signature pages did not state what the signatures acknowledged. Instead, both separate signature pages were later appended to a document that read all four members acknowledged the Final Contract Sale Agreement per their meeting as board members of C.E. LLC. The document date was penciled in at the top of the first page by an unknown source.

C.E.'s signature wasn't intended that he was acknowledging the Final Contract Sale Agreement. Instead, he believed that he was accepting a seat on the board of C.E. LLC based on what Kaka advised his signature meant. It makes one wonder why the document wasn't completed on the day of the asset sale. Wonder no more. A very good reason and likely the only reason, was that Green and Steele were learning every day how they would take all of C.E. Inc., not just its assets, which they hadn't yet figured out on the day of the asset sale. So, in the meantime, they devised a scheme that projected to the world and to C.E. himself that the Final Contract Sale Agreement was completed on the date of the asset sale, and that C.E. acknowledged such a document. How in the world could C.E. acknowledge the Final Contract Sale Agreement as an actual closing document when it wasn't shown to him on the sale date set by the bank? Even so, acknowledging is one thing—reviewing, approving, and signing is yet a whole other breed of cat, and C.E. didn't meet that animal until years later.

But first, they baited their hook very well. A few days before signing the contract sale agreement framework document, C.E. LLC offered C.E. a consulting agreement. It stated that C.E. would serve on the company's board of directors for $100,000.00 a year plus $1000 a day for consultant services. The agreement also specified C.E. would receive up to a certain amount of their contract winnings as an incentive bonus annually at the end of the year.

C.E. hedged on signing with C.E. LLC. It wasn't that good of a contract, given the number of pending award contracts that C.E. Inc. had achieved during his leadership of the company. And he was not keen on working with Green, Steele, and Kaka. The more he was around them, the more he was troubled about their unknown past business practices and how his/our future might be impacted if he did join their newly formed company. But Sneek—the devil's messenger and tool—urged C.E. to sign. Repeating his siren song: "You'll be on the board and earn as much, if not more, as you did as president and CEO of your company. What's not to like?"

Though the consulting agreement from C.E. LLC wasn't close to C.E.'s salary as the president and CEO of C.E. Inc., he thought his other options were limited and went ahead and signed the document. In retrospect, C.E. held the upper hand in the selling of company's assets. He had a two-year contract remaining with his company and had close to $50 million in pending contracts that didn't belong to C.E. LLC. Because of those large federal contracts, he had tremendous untapped leverage.

C.E. tried to exercise this leverage by advising the bank, his company officers, and the officers of C.E. LLC that he would not sign the contract sale agreement framework document until he was separated from his remaining two-year contract with his company, as stipulated in the agreement to collect his severance of almost $1.3 million. But his attempt lost steam when Sneek assured C.E. that he needn't do that because he would be a part of the new company's board of directors. He added that the bank would not pay him his severance in any case because they didn't have to. In his attempt to secure our financial future, C.E. calculated the board seat was much more valuable in the long run because from that position, he thought he would be able to obtain other consulting contract work and serve on the boards of other companies.

Regardless of whether the bank paid C.E. his severance, C.E. LLC was legally required to novate or subcontract all of C.E. Inc.'s active contracts at the time of sale totaling, at least $1 million to $2 million in value. At the minimum, C.E. LLC should have been required by the federal agency's contract specialist holding those contracts to provide the information confirming they could perform on those contracts, C.E. LLC should also have been required to provide a complete application page for each affected contract, showing the transferee as the applicant entity, including its own federally-assigned proprietary number. In any standard federal contract practice, each page would have been signed by both entities, but such a document didn't exist.

To be recognized as the successor in interest, C.E. LLC was required to meet each ongoing contract program eligibility requirement. The pending contracts totaling almost $50 million were not awarded at the time of the asset sale. Thus, technically, they could not be considered a part of the asset sale and did not belong to C.E. LLC. But the Final Contract Sale Agreement, a document that C.E. did not sign and did not see until four years after the asset sale, included language that all future contracts belonged to the C.E. LLC and asserted that C.E. had signed over all those contracts to them by signing the Final Contract Sale Agreement. C.E. would not have signed that document for many reasons, the main one being he did not have the authority to hand over any pending federal contracts. That authority fell to the contracting federal agency to recompete all pending contracts. The C.E. LLC company would have to submit a proposal and compete for the largest pending contract, worth $30 million. That was a risk. What if they didn't win the contract?

Had C.E. played hardball, the C.E. LLC company would have been forced to negotiate a decent and more legally binding contract with him. But C.E. didn't do so because he was led to believe by Green and Steele, and the bank and Sneek, that he would be a part of the new company and would be well compensated. They further advised C.E. that once that was accomplished, they would work with him to help novate or subcontract all current and pending contract bid awards made to C.E. Inc. to C.E. LLC.

But the more he met with the executives of C.E. LLC, the more C.E. became suspicious of their intentions. In the beginning, they treated him respectfully. But as the sale date got closer, Horace Steele became condescending to C.E., to the point of humiliating him. During one of the sale meetings, Steele and the proposed president of the new company, Gustavo Feo, a former military man himself who had zero experience in running an industrial company such as C.E.'s, were overheard talking about C.E.

"Do you think he's afraid?" Steele asked Feo.

"He's afraid, but not of us," responded Feo, chuckling.

There were other hints that the C.E. LLC would not keep C.E. on as president of the new company. In one meeting, Horace Steele told C.E., "We need a young and energetic guy to take over the new company. Someone that can come in early in the morning and leave late at night." C.E. had been doing that for more than seven years and was in excellent health at the time but that didn't seem to matter to the new owners. They were finding every excuse to get rid of him.

It became clearer and clearer that Green, Steele, and Kaka intended to take the entire company from C.E. the minute they figured out how do it. And C.E. made it easy for them to dump him without too much effort. He was cooperating with them so the sell could go through smoothly, signing one document after another while not raising questions. His main reason for being so ready with the pen had to do with the bank's threat to sue him and with C.E. wanting to get paid something—anything— that the C.E. LLC company offered until he found employment elsewhere. Being honorable should be a winning characteristic in human behavior. But, in C.E.'s case, it proved fatal in his dealings regarding his company's asset sale. He believed Green, Steele and Kaka, at the beginning. The aggressive way they courted him to join their company's board of directors gave him every reason to sign all documents by wielding the proverbial 'carrot and stick.' His continued fear of the bank's threat to sue him if he didn't sign the sale documents, along with his two officers demanding he sign the framework document and the new company's offer of a board seat, consulting fees, and bonus at the end of the year, led C.E. to make decisions he deeply regretted later. He didn't believe they were capable of being that dishonest and conniving.

During the end of the sale process, C.E. became highly suspicious of their motives and grew even more concerned but by that time it was too late. He confronted Steele when he encountered him walking down the hallway in his company's executive area. "What the fuck is going on here anyway?" C.E. demanded.

Steele nearly jumped out of his skin, surprised that C.E. had shed his gentlemanly shell. "Ahhhh, the bank is not without blood on its hands either!" Steele nervously replied as he walked away hastily from C.E., bumping into several people along the way. The sale was on, and there was very little or nothing C.E. could do to change that. C.E. had run out of runway.

About a couple of weeks after C.E. signed the incomplete framework of the Contract Sale Agreement, he got dressed to attend the first board meeting of the C.E. LLC company. He was the happiest I had seen him in a long time. As he exited out the front door he said, "It'll be great to see the company's employees." The company's workforce was primarily made up of men and women from the northern triangle—Guatemala, Honduras, and El Salvador. Hard-working people, many of whom supported not only their families but other extended family members. He liked them very much and appreciated their hard work and dedication to the company. The employees, in turn, showed their respect and admiration for C.E.'s leadership on many occasions. On one day, practically every employee stood in line to personally thank C.E. for his decision to have the company pay for their health benefits.

But the day of the first board meeting, C.E. never made it to his old company. Instead, Kaka called him midway in route and asked to meet him at a restaurant instead. Charlie sat comfortably in his chair, sipping a cup of tea when C.E. arrived. After the usual greetings, Charlie wasted no time telling C.E. that he and the other board members were dismissing him from the board. "They don't want you to be a part of the board," he explained. "They're going to talk about your management style, and you won't like what they'll have to say."

C.E.'s heart sank. He saw everything he worked for after retiring from the Army go up in smoke. He expected a lot of things from Kaka, but not this. As he tried to compose himself from revealing his disappointment, Kaka rubbed salt in the wound when he announced: "Oh, by the way, we're lowering your $100,000 consulting agreement to $40,000. Take it or leave it."

If C.E. was such a poor manager, why did the C.E. LLC company offer him a consulting agreement in the first place? Because they never intended to have him serve as part of the new company. It was all smoke and mirrors. They cooked up the consulting agreement as a ruse, a bait-and-switch, to have him in turn sign a framework of a document they called a Contract Sale Agreement that would authorize C.E. Inc. to sell all of its assets to C.E. LLC. All the officers of C.E. LLC wanted was C.E.'s signature on the Contract Sale Agreement framework document, along with that of Gustavo Feo's, the president and CEO of C.E. LLC, so they could insert the page with both signatures into the Final Version of the Contract Sale Agreement which they didn't share with C.E. then or ever. In doing so, it would appear to the world that C.E. signed such a document, which did not happen but which allowed the C.E. LLC company a huge opening to take all of C.E. Inc., not just its assets, while C.E. got nothing in return.

The C.E. LLC company was fully aware it inherited a well-trained and dedicated workforce, led by C.E. There were no EEO or labor-related or on-the-job injury complaints. Under C.E.'s watch, C.E. Inc. had been pre-awarded close to $50 million in pending contracts and so much of that was based on the quality products produced by the dedicated and skilled workforce.

But back to Kaka's offer to C.E. at the restaurant. "Take it or leave it" is the oldest negotiator's bullying tactic around, and it works well with a con when one party is fearful of the other. And the guy that once was the formidable war planner and multiple military medal awardee fell for it. C.E. signed the amended page that Kaka presented to him.

On his way home, C.E. called me and could barely speak. "It's not good," he said softly. He was a dispirited soul when he walked in the front door of our warm and happy home that soon became a place of immense despair. After a few minutes, he gained his composure long enough to tell me what Charlie had told him.

"You didn't sign the document? Tell me you didn't sign it?" I asked anxiously. He lowered his head, saying nothing.

A few days later, Charlie sent him yet another amendment. This time, the daily rate of $1,000 was reduced to $500 and the incentive bonus was omitted. C.E. signed it and was even gracious. "Thanks, Charlie," he wrote.

This time, the C.E. LLC reduced the $500 daily consultant rate to an amount "to be determined." C.E. felt it was best for him to cooperate with the C.E. LLC leadership, to ensure he had some income until finding other employment. At that point, I saw the train wreck that would upend our once financially secure life. While C.E., the eternal optimist, thought we'd come out okay. In the end, C.E. ended up with a document that paid him only $40,000 and nothing more.

In comparison, C.E. LLC purportedly paid only $3.4 million into C.E. Inc.'s loan with the bank, which had a balance of approximately $6 million. This arrangement between the bank and C.E. LLC is questionable since the bank didn't seek the approval of C.E. Inc.'s three officers. This arrangement also allowed for C.E. LLC to convince itself and the world that they had bought all of C.E. Inc., not just its assets.

In a conversation with Pancho O'Grady shortly after the asset sale, Gustavo Feo laughingly said, "We bought the whole enchilada!" Pancho was taken aback. He asked himself how that could have happened since all three officers only signed over the assets of C.E. Inc. and nothing more. After years of working in the federal contract business, Pancho was aware that, when another company such as the C.E. LLC company is allowed by a bank to pay into another company's loan, this doesn't result in ownership of the entire company, especially when the entire loan is not paid and especially when several legal documents are floating around stating that C.E. LLC only bought C.E. Inc.'s assets, not the entity. C.E. LLC ran roughshod over C.E. Inc. It unabashedly took its federally-assigned proprietary number and masqueraded as if it was one and the same company, falsely portraying itself as having years of experience in the industrial field, which it had zero years. It was a company literally made up overnight. But by the bank opening the door for C.E. LLC to take all of C.E. Inc., and their willingness to forego following federal acquisition regulations, they ended up with C.E. Inc's federal proprietary number which was worth millions.

Approximately fifteen months after purchasing C.E. Inc's assets for a pittance, C.E. LLC sold itself to a larger Midwest company listed to trade on the Over-The-Counter (OTC) market, for $50 million. It's important to understand that OTC (or off-exchange) trading is done directly between two parties without an exchange's supervision. In an OTC trade, the price is not necessarily publicly disclosed. Each party could have credit risk concerns regarding the other party. The OTC market does not have the safety measures of a traditional stock exchange (like the New York Stock Exchange) to ensure the quality of the financial instruments bought and sold and the credibility of the parties involved. Such a market as the OTC was a perfect environment for those involved in forcing the sale of C.E. Inc's assets and those that bought it. Any sales or acquisition news for many OTC-listed companies enables the stock price to be pumped up, even if only for a short period for profit taking by shareholders.

C.E. Inc's asset sale became a tragic comedy of errors for C.E. His actions remind me of my favorite lawyer stories. This famous lawyer was a colorful, brilliant litigator who represented women who killed their husbands in self-defense. The lawyer represented three dozen such women during his career once said: "I won all but two of those cases. And I would have won them if my clients hadn't kept reloading their gun and firing."

Had I been a lawyer, no matter how good at my craft, C.E's decision to sign one amended consulting agreement after another did not differ from the two women represented by the famous lawyer who lost. C.E. kept reloading and firing by signing by document after another. But he did it to protect himself and his family, only to still end up on the losing side.

I couldn't excuse C.E.'s behavior. For many months after the sale of C.E. Inc.'s assets, it was difficult for me to sit or lay next to him. We were close to splitting up, something I never dreamed would be possible. I always felt that our marriage could withstand any catastrophe, any world event or personal issues that spun around us. But C.E.'s part in allowing himself to be left with a few thousand dollars made it harder and harder for me to swallow the "Till Death Do Us Part" pill.

In his defense, C.E. trusted others who once wore a military uniform, believing them to be honest and transparent in dealing with him about their proposal to buy his company's assets and their offer of a board seat with their new company. He cooperated with them from beginning to end about everything, from warmly welcoming Green and Steele into his office, allowing them to use hard-to-get front door parking, briefing them in great detail about the company's pending and pre-awarded contracts, allowing them to stay as long as they wanted to conduct their due diligence, signing one document after another, while he got kicked in the teeth by Green, Steele, and Kaka, tossing him out on the street without regard for his well-being, his future, and that of his family. In a word, they were godless.

When Kaka came to C.E. with the "take it or leave it proposition," he interpreted that to mean sign or you get nothing. C.E. feared that ending up with zero money would cripple us financially forever. He did not want to risk that by fighting back. To him, the $40,000 would keep us afloat until he found other employment, or until I did. But that was a pipe dream on his part. He was a 78-year-old man who had just sold his company for an embarrassingly low amount in the eyes of the world. How that happened and how he lost his position within the company would be irrelevant to the outside world. His marketable days were pretty much over.

Me, I am not wired that way. I'm not that trusting and would have shoved the consulting agreement amendment up Kaka's ass one page at a time. And for good measure, I would have threatened to sue the lying bastard and the rest of the equally lying C.E. LLC company board members if they didn't honor the original contract. But we humans are all made of different stock. It's up to us to respect one another based on those differences and not be critical. I've worked hard to accept that. But as time went on, I realized C.E. knew very little about what was happening around him before and after his company's asset sale because the parties involved kept him blindfolded during the entire sale process, while reassuring him that his place in the new company was secure. The moral of this story: Pay attention to everything that's happening around you. Ask questions, don't take anything for granted, and don't trust anyone unless they earn it.

When C.E. first met Simon Green and Horace Steele, they seemed friendly and ordinary working folks. But he noticed that they drove beat-up old cars—not what you'd expect from two people in a position to pay for his company's assets and to demonstrate their ability to fund the operation of a fast-tracked industrial company. Their wardrobe was no better: outdated suits and worn, scuffed, dirty shoes. That was then: now, Simon Green and Charlie Kaka formed another company with modern offices and ride around in shiny new cars with a matching expensive wardrobe. Gustavo Feo left the presidency of C.E. LLC to start his own company. Other key employees went off to join other companies or form their own entities. And Horace Steele, for a while, became a key executive with the company that bought C.E. LLC. He is currently the president and CEO of a major company, works in other companies, and is still connected to the company that bought C.E. LLC. He lives in a multi-million-dollar home in one of the most exclusive neighborhoods in the country.

During the early purchase of C.E. LLC, the Midwest company's stock was around $4.00 and had not necessarily made a profit from their acquisition of the company. However, a few years ago, they received a multi-million dollar contract from the federal government in a no-bid, unsolicited federal award that was obtained through the federally-assigned number that belonged to C.E. Inc. During that time, their stock jumped to $35. It made the news and not in a good way. After that, their stock tanked and is now trading in single digits once again.

While Simon Green, Horace Steele, and Charlie Kaka successfully sold their company for millions, C.E. and I lost our beloved home in the city to foreclosure. We sold most of our goods, depleted all our savings, and now reside in what used to be our weekend retreat—a home we live in but don't own in any way, shape, or form. We remain in debt. Not new debt, but the same old bills we had when C.E. lost his job.

Chapter 4
The Ship Sinks

"Everything that happens is meant to be. It's meant to happen like that. But sometimes you don't know at the time that it's meant to be a disaster."— Tony Kaye

Some people lose their wealth to an obsessive gambling habit. Others lose it to being unlucky or through unwise investments, and others to careless spending. Then some work hard for the pot, only to lose it to someone cleverer.

Any time there is a congressional sequester, the government shuts down, which tends to produce a financial situation across the country ripe for hostile takeovers of companies by vultures (both individuals and corporate) who specialize in quasi-legal theft. That untimely financial situation created the conditions C.E. and I suffered (and still suffer) because it made his company vulnerable. My husband lost all his potential wealth because he believed that the incentive of working with businesses to make a profit would trump all else for financial institutions. Unfortunately, his healthy dose of natural naïveté made him guilty of being too trusting in that widely held and misperceived motivation. Some institutions—like banks and investors—can also make money from a company losing money. This is especially true if it leads to a situation—whether inadvertent or intentional—that creates a false assumption of the value of the company's assets. In our case, this idea never received enough consideration. And out of fear of retribution, C.E. Inc's asset value was never contested—instead, a better offer was never negotiated. Perhaps no deal was ever made because of the low offer.

C.E. was a career military man. Like most people in the military, he reentered the civilian business world woefully unprepared for how devastatingly different the culture and environment of civilian life can be from the one he had always known. The career military person, officer or enlisted, is used to receiving and giving orders to be carried out at once. If there is a discussion, it doesn't last for hours. A decision is made, executed, and the chain of command held accountable. The military lives by Duty, Honor, and Country, as do most veterans once they've left the service. Things simply get done because of the tangible honesty by which they live and work. It's perverse to frame those positive qualities in this way, but it's the truth. My husband has those traits and, in the sale of C.E. Inc.'s assets, trusting in those instincts brought us to a financial collapse that we have yet to recover from.

Losing money, wealth, and the more intangible riches of reputation and respect is nothing new. One of our country's first Presidents died in debt, having spent much of his money on rare, expensive wines from France and other things. Poor investments caused a former NFL player to lose over $50 million and forced him to declare bankruptcy. A lottery winner of $113 million after taxes ended up broke. The list goes on and on... men and women, educated and non-educated, who have lost their entire fortunes.

C.E.'s case was and is different. He had built a successful industrial business but, because of accounting technicalities, the timing of political and economic events, and a lender's desire to sell the company at a loss to heartless and duplicitous characters not only did he lose his income as company president and CEO but he also lost equity that would have increased in value based on future revenue from the contracts the company would be awarded. That would have resulted in millions of dollars for us. C.E. and I went from being in the one percent of high-income earners to part of the 95 percent of low-income Americans. And when that happened, it sent both of us into financial collapse and a world of utter despair.

All things considered, at first we thought we would be able to weather the storm. And the experience was akin to being on a ship at sea: once comfortably sailing in serene waters, but suddenly we were in rough weather that grew increasingly worse and, just as suddenly, our vessel began leaking. It took on more water as it thrashed about on an angry sea. So it was for us. Less and less money came into our household to keep us afloat. It seemed everything was working against us. The dark angel of misfortune broke into our home and refused to leave.

Just as we thought things couldn't get any worse, our financial woes multiplied. One day, we were paying to repair the brakes on one of our cars; the next, we bought new tires for another vehicle. And yet, on another day, we were forced to replace a blown-up heating and air conditioner system. There were other unforeseen expenses on the horizon. C.E. needed significant dental work, as did our poodle, Zippy whose teeth had to be constantly cleaned and, in some cases, extracted. Both ended up with permanent damage to their teeth. Zippy died from gum disease and other teeth-related problems. We simply weren't bringing in enough money to pay for the high dental costs. Hell, we couldn't even feed ourselves. We had no food in the house at one low point and divided three cans of tuna among us. And in one embarrassing moment, we bought more at the grocery store than we had money to pay for. It was the most painful and humiliating experience having to put some food items back on the shelf.

In past years, our earnings allowed us to pay our bills on time and to help those close to us and donate to charities. But our retirement income simply couldn't stretch far enough to pay for all the bills we had before C.E. lost his job. For our formerly 'good' life to end suddenly was simply unthinkable. It brought me to my knees. I couldn't eat and couldn't sleep. My heart would begin racing of its own accord, faster, faster, faster until I was sure it would burst and send me to an early grave. It was, and still is, an unimaginably doomed feeling of despair and death.

The further into debt we sank, the worse my anxiety became, sending me deeper into darkness. During my early pre-menopause years, I suffered severe anxiety attacks. They went away once my hormonal level balanced itself, but they were torturous years. In a similar vein, I lost all sense of control over my mind in dealing with our financial losses and bleak future. Only through prayer and faith did I begin to take control of my feelings.

We were forced to sell practically all our possessions to stay afloat. Our choices of what to sell or donate weren't as simple as they might seem. It was a horror of a nightmare to sort through so much of our life's acquisitions and nearly impossible to be emotionally prepared to part with them. Never in my wildest dreams could I have imagined I'd end up in this type of financial wreck. We were sinking toward the bottom… and neither of us saw a way up.

To cope, I had to remind myself we weren't alone in selling almost everything we owned. Many others had been in the same boat and survived. I thought about a former Texas governor who sold many of his life's possessions. However, his fate had been tied to bad investments in the oil market, not having a bank selling off his well-run company.

I thought that comparing our disastrous financial situation to someone else's would make the pain less severe—but it didn't. In his workbook *Get Out of Your Mind & Into Your Life*, Steven C. Hayes explains that loss is a state of 'what once was.' He theorizes people can transform their emotional pain into something useful. In my case, none of this applied. The mental anguish was too severe for me to get under control. I entered a dark tunnel that seemed to have no end and I could not find my way out.

When things go wrong, it's easier to blame everyone around you than to examine yourself. Here, I felt C.E.—my very own husband—was to blame for what had happened to us. At first, it seemed we faced these circumstances because of decisions C.E. made on his own…not with me. And the more I thought about it, the more unlikely it became—in my mind—that we would face our penniless future together. I did not see any way we could remain together, and that might have been the harshest pain of all. Yet, my love for C.E. was deep and everlasting. I knew that level of love for one another would sustain our marriage.

I don't recall what incident brought me back into C.E.'s arms. Perhaps it was the incessant phone calls from creditors (I needed someone to share the humiliation) or the possibility of losing all our belongings. I honored the wedding vow 'for richer or poorer' that I had taken almost thirty-five years earlier. It rang in my mind like a chant from above that struck a renewed and positive chord in our relationship. We reunited and began the long process of fighting the battles we faced together.

Bankruptcy became the simple answer to our growing fear of losing everything we possessed. It was a thought I dreaded more than anything in the world. Bankruptcy is like a scarlet letter that remains stamped upon your identity. Bad credit only lasts seven years; bankruptcy can follow you to your grave. Only irresponsible people filed for bankruptcy… or so I used to think. Of course, that was not the case, and it wasn't our situation. I've now learned that bad things happen to good people who don't deserve them.

When C.E. lost his mid-six-figure job, we suffered severe consequences in every aspect of our lives. Not a single dollar we were bringing in from retirement accounts seemed to ease our financial problems. Our retirement incomes weren't enough to make ends meet. Our credit card debt went to collections when we could no longer afford to make the minimum payments. Our negative credit report alone seemed enough to make a person jump off the nearest tall building, as many did during America's Great Depression in the 1930s. You couldn't make this shit up if you tried!

We were at our wit's end, so we decided to reach out for advice to our dear friend Ed Johnson who had filed for bankruptcy some years before. We met him at a McDonald's, the only place any of us could afford to meet. Our conversation centered on Ed's financial crisis rather than ours. His situation was like C.E.'s. He had been fired from his position as president of a nonprofit in an overnight decision. However, Ed's situation was worse than C.E.'s, if that was even possible. He didn't have retirement income to fall back on and he and his wife had three adopted children. They lost everything, including a lovely and spacious house. They now live in a trailer in an RV park.

We asked our friend what he felt he had done wrong during his recovery. He responded that he should have filed for bankruptcy way before he did. It was a surprising answer, but one we heard often. He had no choice but to do what it took to protect his family's welfare. And strange as it sounds, it was comforting to hear his story. We weren't the only ones in trouble, I reminded myself… as if that was going to improve our lot.

He warned us to expect incessant calls from creditors. At the same time, he urged us not to be afraid of or be intimidated by the collection agents who would soon become an unwelcome part of our lives. He admitted that their incessant calls were enough to lead anyone to go completely mad. "But not me," he said proudly. "I simply tell them to fuck off and hang up the phone." But even I knew that, as earthy as I had the potential to be, it wouldn't be wise for me to take his advice. It was in my interest to appease our creditors, not antagonize them.

Diplomacy took over. I found myself engaged in tearful conversations with those who were once arrogant and impatient bill collectors. They worked with us. Some deferred the due dates on our payments, giving us more time to pay. Others took lower payments, and a few even prayed with me, asking for God's blessings upon us. Many times, both the collection agent and I hung up weeping. Still, we were slipping farther and farther behind.

C.E. and I eagerly followed our friend's advice and pressed on to find and meet with a bankruptcy lawyer. When we found one through Google, I went kicking and screaming to our appointment. The last thing I wanted in my life was the "B" letter planted on my forehead forever. But C.E. and I felt we had no way out of the financial disaster we found ourselves in. When we arrived at the lawyer's address, we stepped away, thinking we had the wrong address. It didn't seem like anyone lived in the building from its appearance. But the lawyer did have his office in the weather-beaten townhouse that resembled a set design from a horror movie: grass taller than me, broken window shutters, glass windows that didn't seem to have had a splash of Windex in years, and a front door that screeched to high heaven when we pulled it open.

The smell of dampness and years-old mold swept over me as we stepped into the lawyer's tiny office. I wondered what kind of rating the Bar Association gave this unassuming man. He seemed young enough to be our grandson and worked alone with no staff. He was dressed in clothes that seemed to have come from the donation bins at the Salvation Army. Nothing about his appearance indicated we were about to sit down with a bright, sophisticated law school graduate who would help us find our way in and out of bankruptcy court. In the end, he turned out to be a much better legal advisor than fashion aficionado.

After hearing our story, he cut to the chase. "You don't qualify for bankruptcy protection because you own nothing," he said. "Not only that, but you also live on retirement income, and no one can take that from you. So, don't sweat it."

C.E. and I stared at each other in surprise. I felt a slight stirring of relief. "But what about all the creditors demanding payment?" I asked.

"Let 'em stand in line," the lawyer said matter-of-factly, adding, "You don't have to pay them if you don't want to." He assured us that no one could take away our retirement income and we could do with it what we felt more important. He added that filing for bankruptcy was out of the question since we didn't own anything.

In less than fifteen minutes, C.E. and I were out of the lawyer's office clutching each other's hands, thinking we'd been freed. While our elation had to do with not being forced to file for bankruptcy, sadly, it was all for the wrong reasons. The lawyer surmised we didn't have a pot to piss in, and that touched a raw nerve in both of us. That day, the only good news was that the lawyer didn't charge us to meet with him. Instead, he showed compassion, something not even some of the people we considered friends had shown us. We had told no one of our woes, but those closest to us realized we were about to go over a cliff of unpaid—unpayable—debt. Yet, they didn't offer to help us. At one point, one of our friends said: "I wish I knew how I could help." C.E. and I pretended not to hear her. But under my breath, I said, *"How about loaning us $25? That would buy us much-needed food around here."* To be fair, we didn't want to lean on any of our friends, rich or poor to help relief our financial stress. Things were embarrassing enough for C.E. and me without having to borrow large amounts of money from close friends that we didn't know whether we could ever pay them back. So, while they didn't write us a check, our friends did all they could to uplift our spirits. Two of our closest friends, Beatrice and Klaus Schmidt went the extra mile, inviting us to their home on weekends to keep us from literally falling apart. My advice to those who ever find themselves in similar circumstances is to expect not one thing from anyone including your own relatives. Allow yourself to be surprised by their expression of love and support which in the end is more relevant than money.

About this time, I began listening to ads from companies that help people consolidate their debt. We fell into this category but not because we were spending irresponsibly. In our case, we had existing bills that our retirement income couldn't cover. The message from the consolidation companies seemed easy and inviting, but I learned they charged hefty fees to help merge all your bills into one large one. I thought, *Why pay someone else for something I can do myself?* So, I planned with each of our creditors to make monthly payments based on our retirement income level and what we could afford. I became the keeper of our household budget, making sure it was balanced to the penny at the end of each month. It worked, but it didn't raise our credit rating—if anything, our credit kept getting lower and lower.

Even though C.E. and I had been advised to forget about paying our bills, we had no plans to run from our financial obligations. While I successfully made payment arrangements with our creditors, it differed with our car payments. Banks typically don't refinance existing car loans unless your credit score is at least 700. If somehow you manage to find a lender that will refinance, they'll charge you an arm and a leg in interest rates. Unfortunately for us, our credit had suffered almost immediately after C.E. lost his job. And a credit rating is the cornerstone of any household's financial standing and future. It defines you and sets limits or becomes an unbreakable barrier. In our case, a low credit rating prevented us from many things we could have done easily in previous years.

Still, our two vehicles had to be paid for, or else they'd be repossessed. We were stuck with both because their value had depreciated, and we could not sell them at the price that we still owed on them.

We were forced to borrow from two family members and a long-time friend. It was a humiliating experience to ask for the help but neither C.E. nor I saw any other way out. Had it not been for them and my work as a consultant, we would have lost both vehicles and a lot more. And we had no possibility of buying or even renting another, given our credit score. The last thing we wanted was to borrow from anyone. But we thought a settlement would be around the corner, and we could pay them back quickly. But no settlement came so it took us a long time to pay back the loans which didn't sit well with our lenders. My advice is that no matter how down-and-out you find yourself, try your best not to borrow from friends or family. Today only one of those that lent us the money still speaks to us.

When we came so close to losing our vehicles, I couldn't help but think of the REPO show on television. Once, it had been hysterically funny to watch the repossession agents chasing after vehicle owners who were determined to keep their cars from being driven away. Now, the show was no longer a laughing matter. Finding yourself inches away from being chased in the same way changes your perspective. The idea of having anything repossessed was as foreign to me as believing that pigs fly.

The only people I knew who'd had their car repossessed were the parents of my high school friend. I still remember when it happened:

"Bonita, I lost my car," my friend's mother cried when I entered their beautiful spacious home one summer evening. Instead of enjoying the delicious meal my friend's mother had prepared, our small group sat around the dining table, crying, and carrying on, mourning the loss of their Ford station wagon. We comforted each other while reminiscing about our experiences riding in the car. One such story brought our group to hilarious laughter, a therapeutic relief we badly needed. The story was about a group of young college students from Mexico visiting our hometown during *Semana Santa* (Holy Week). My friend and I were riding around the city when we encountered a group of six young men at the stoplight. They were heavenly cute, and the flirting began. But as my friend prepared to drive off when the green light came on, all six men tried to physically stop our car, holding on to its door handles and open windows. My friend wanted to slow down to allow them time to release themselves from the vehicle but instead pressed on the accelerator, dragging all of them along the city's busiest street. They looked like bowling pins bouncing up and down the town's busiest shopping street.

The family's only transportation loss shocked me. They were viewed as having more than most on the Mexican side of town, but when I told my mother about the loss, she didn't seem surprised, nor did she care. *"Esa gente no tenen nada, proque no trabajan,"* she said sarcastically: "These people have nothing because they do not work."

"I thought they were rich," I said innocently.

"*Que ricos ni que ricos, esa gente no tenen en que caerse muertos,*" my mother replied sarcastically. Her words surprised me, saying my friend's family wasn't rich and, if they died, didn't have money to be given a decent burial.

"Can we help them get their car back?" I pleaded.

"*Eres una pendeja, nadie vay ajudar a esa gente por que se crean muy grande,*" my mother responded in her tone that conveyed how stupid I was. She declared no one would help them because that family thought they were better than the rest of us in the *barrio*. Mother was right, maybe not for the reason she cited, but she was right. No one helped my friend's parents keep their car from being repo'd…and no one helped them try to purchase another less expensive car. It was sad to witness a once happy family turn into one full of despair. Little did I know that, one day, I would share their feelings at the time and, by a mere hair's breadth, would not end up in their shoes.

As our finances unraveled, we tried our best to hold on. But we couldn't. Everything bad that could happen began happening. We entered a dark period in our lives, which could have been totally avoidable had the bank given C.E. and his two officers the same business opportunity it did to C.E. LLC, or had Green, Steele and Kaka honored their original consulting agreement with C.E. It started with our homes and went south from there. We no longer had the income to pay for two mortgages. We thought of opening a GoFundMe account to find the cash to pay our mounting legal bills, get our accounts out of collections, and save our city home. But neither C.E. nor I could see us panhandling over the internet. We figured that somehow, some way, we'd get enough money to pay everyone we owed. We still thought there would be a settlement with the people who had taken over C.E.'s business and the company that hadn't paid his severance.

It never happened.

We decided to sell our primary home in the city and keep our country home. We figured it would yield a bigger return in the future. Unfortunately, our home in the city was under water. The mortgage was greater than its value, and it never sold, even at the price we were forced to list it at. In desperation, we applied and were approved for a modification loan to reduce our monthly mortgage payment. Still, we couldn't afford to keep the city home, even at the lower payment.

Our beautiful and beloved home in the city, where we had lived for over twenty-five years, where we had entertained friends and associates from royalty to members of the President's cabinet, was foreclosed on. My heart sank and felt like it was broken into tiny pieces when I saw the 'Foreclosure' sign on our front lawn. The same yard we decorated every Halloween night, sending small children scurrying with screams of joy and mock fear of the many ghosts and goblins strategically placed. The same lawn we decorated every Christmas season, where neighbors and visitors stopped to admire the festive display.

The whispers of neighbors sharing gossip about our downfall were hard to ignore. From our kitchen window, we could see them walking past our home, pointing toward it, and shaking their heads. No one, but no one, offered so much as a shoulder to lean on, a cup of coffee, or a plate of food. Not even a biscuit for our Zippy. That's what happens when bad things occur. No one wants to come near you because they fear your bad luck will rub off on them. It became a dark and isolated world for C.E. and me.

Before the foreclosure, we were forced to sell most of our furniture, clothing, jewelry, and other items that had been a special part of our thirty-five years of marriage. We choked back tears as one item after another was carried out and put into some stranger's vehicle.

There were certain unique jewelry pieces I at first refused to part with that represented special times during our marriage. But eventually, they too had to be given up. The power company sent us a warning letter saying we would be cut off if we didn't pay the bill by a specific date. And it would cost $300 to restore electricity, plus late fee charges. So, I frantically drove to a pawn shop near our home and gave up a gold elephant pendant C.E. had gifted me many years earlier on a snowy Christmas Day. One of my favorite pieces, the elephant with its trunk raised, was supposed to represent good luck. But, I thought, *So much for good luck… look what's happened*. So, finally, after weeks of agonizing over its loss, I returned to the pawnshop to retrieve it.

"Sorry," the store clerk said, "it was melted down along with the other gold pieces you brought in." I started weeping in front of the clerk. "I am sorry, ma'am, but that's what happens to gold in our pawn shop; I thought you knew that."

I whispered under my breath, "How the hell am I supposed to know that… I've never in my life stepped into a fricking pawnshop." So, my specially gifted pendant was erased forever, just as was our previous life. Nothing was going to bring it back. That was so difficult to understand and accept. Our life, as we once knew it, was over. Finished. Kaput! Our next challenge was to navigate the subsequent phase in our financially-crippled lives. It was a daunting question that haunted both of us every minute—every single day and every single night.

And I thought of my mother.

She always managed to hold on to her money, and the bills were always paid on time. When my mother passed away, she had three different active bank accounts, two homes, and a brand-new car. She had no outstanding bills and left her four surviving children with a modest but decent inheritance.

At 68 years old, I found myself Ivy League trained in public management having served in several corporate and government senior-level management positions, broke beyond belief. My assets were few to none, no job in the offing, and an ever-mounting stack of bills to pay. An unbelievable and embarrassing state of affairs. I figured my mother was not rolling in her grave, she was doing double and triple summersaults, while yelling, *"Que esperan, esa gente son un bola de ladrones and mentirosos. Por que no se los han chingado?*—What are you waiting for, those people are a bunch of thieves and liars. Why haven't you and your husband fucked them over?

Chapter 5

Collateral Damage

"If the price of collateral damage is high
enough, you might be able to get paid
for bringing ammunition home with you."
*The Seventy Maxims of Maximally Effective
Mercenaries* – Howard Tayler

My mother, bless her soul, was always missing in action when I needed her most. A fiercely independent woman, Lola marched to the beat of her own drum. She was a fearless soul who was intimidated by no one. Not even the bigoted ruling class Anglos scared her off like they did other minorities in my hometown, a sleepy, mid-size town located near the ocean on the west coast. Growing up there was often pleasant, at least as much as I could hope for, given the marginalized life I led. Anglos lived on one side of town, Mexicans on the other side, and Blacks were confined to a small area of land north of town.

Mother didn't look nor act like the rest of "Las Comadres," as women in our neighborhood referred to one another. She rejected the term "Comadre." It denoted gossipy women my mother often complained about. Maybe my mother's Spanish-Jewish roots on her father's side separated her from the rest of the lot on the town's south side. No one in our family talked about my maternal grandfather's past— after all, he had been baptized a Catholic in Mexico.

When I was about ten or eleven years old, I heard two old men talking on the street in front of my grandparent's house. One of them pointed to my grandparent's house and said in a loud voice: *"A mi parese que Don Daniel es Judeo."* The stranger's words made me wince. My grandfather was what? *Un Judeo*? What did *Judeo* mean? I wrestled with the man's words for days. In the end, I chose not to say anything about it to a household full of paranoid, superstitious, and guilt-ridden folks who never seemed to be happy unless they were gossiping about someone's downfall, including that of members of our own family. Years later, when I learned what *Judeo* meant, I thought that perhaps the men in front of our house were on to something. My grandfather Daniel Goyo never stepped into the Catholic church. The home he shared with my Nanita Lucia was not adorned with makeshift altars decorated with candles worshipping La Virgen de Guadalupe and Jesus, as were so many Mexican homes on the town's south side. Yet I can also say that there were no menorahs or mezuzahs on display anywhere in my grandparent's house, leaving me more confused as I grew older.

Lola worked outside the home while the other women in our neighborhood stayed at home. Their daily routine differed significantly from my mother's. The women spent most of their day confined to tiny kitchen spaces, standing over hot stoves flipping flour tortillas, stirring huge pots of pinto beans while cooking up a beef stew called *guisado*. Along with that unending work, a string of crying children continually tugged at their apron strings.

Mostly, the women were in relationships with apathetic, cranky, dominating men who wouldn't allow them to get a driver's permit, socialize outside their home, or travel anywhere alone without their permission. If they failed to follow their rules, they could expect a beating. They were docile women who weren't allowed to have an original thought. When their men spoke, they listened.

Not my mother, though. She wasn't the do-what-any-man-says type. Lola would stare down anyone that dared look at her cross-eyed. Her reputation for being tough with nerves of steel was well known throughout town. She worked hard and started her day early. She was dressed in a crisp, clean white uniform to begin her short-order cook job by 4:00 am. She was gone before the crack of dawn, and every day I could count on her getting home at 2:00 pm on the dot.

As soon as my mother entered our home, she hurriedly shed the now-soiled white uniform she proudly wore. I followed her to pick it up, wash it in Clorox bleach, which was her obsessive rule, and press it to be ready the next morning. Meanwhile, Lola slipped into one of her many fashionable sundresses, the *de rigueur* stylish wardrobe in our hometown. These dresses also kept you from dropping with heatstroke.

No matter her wardrobe, Lola was sure to accessorize it with her ever-present black leather handbag, which she clutched as if it contained the Hope diamond. Without saying a word, she hurriedly slipped out the back door, racing toward her car, brushing her thick, black curly hair as a Camel cigarette dangled from her ruby red lips. She was off to entertain her boyfriend—a heavily-mustached, slim, and well-to-do man who had been living with his wife and three sons a short time earlier. But thanks to my mother, that family was no longer together.

Don Leopoldo Gonzalez was a well-known entrepreneur and one of the wealthiest in the town's westside. He and Lola fell in love the moment they met when I was six years old. They had a 35-year love affair, never marrying because Lola wanted to stay in her home and run her life as she pleased. Don Leo as he preferred to be called, supplemented my mother's income throughout their affair. My three older half-sisters left home to be married at very early ages, so they never benefitted from the financial security afforded me and my brother. Don Leo took us on trips all over California, bought me my first car that I drove all through high school, provided me with a healthy weekly allowance and paid for the secretarial school I attended after high school. His financial generosity allowed Lola to save most of her earnings which she invested wisely.

Yet, with all the baggage that came with her nature, my mother always made sure all five children were well fed and nicely clothed. She refused to stop working even though Don Leo more than did his share to ensure we were financially secure.

Lola didn't want to be dependent on any man, and didn't want me to be either, she stressed time and time again. So, for over thirty-years, she rose every morning to toil over a hot stove and oven, cooking and baking a large variety of mouth-watering home-cooked style meals and desserts for the townsfolk and the many tourists who traveled through our town to the coastal area. She worked just as hard as her neighbors. The big difference was that Lola was paid for her work at the café and wasn't beaten by the customers if the food didn't taste good.

After she finished her work at the café, Lola was on call to deliver one baby after another. She delivered more babies than I care to count which included delivering her two oldest daughter's first born. While she was at it, Lola helped many a poor young girl terminate their pregnancies that were mostly caused through rape by a relative or by some local married man. When I became of age, I was her secretary, scheduling appointments and collecting fees which Lola typically dismissed since the girls didn't have money to pay for the services.

Mother had enough money with assistance from Don Leo to allow my brother and me to participate in various school programs rarely afforded by our fellow Mexican-American classmates. We were a part of the handful of Mexicans who ate in the school cafeteria, albeit among a sea of unwelcoming white faces. That assistance also allowed us to participate in otherwise unattainable school activities that she preached would make better human beings out of us both. Tennis was my favorite sport, but costly. Lola didn't blink an eye. She paid for everything required of the sport to keep me out of her hair, and I suspect more so than for me to learn to compete. There were no other Mexicans on the school's tennis team, so I leaned on my fast serve and quick reflexes to keep my eye on the ball to impress my Anglo teammates. It worked. They welcomed me into the team, but only up to a point. Competition was one thing, socializing was another. They never invited me into their lives after tennis practice and matches. Racism loomed big in my hometown, in the surrounding towns, and for the entire state as far as I knew. No mixing was allowed among the White folks, Black folks, and Mexicans. After school, all three groups went their separate ways.

For the longest time, I thought my official nicknames were 'Wetback' and 'Dirty Mexican.' That was the way of the world in my hometown. You sucked it up and, if you dared challenge it, you could find yourself being the center of attention for all the wrong reasons. When I was six years old, I defiantly or angrily lofted a gob of my spit on a teenage white girl's face after she called me a dirty Mexican one time too many. Instead of being praised for standing up for myself and my fellow Mexican-American classmates, I was the talk of the school, and not in a good way. Everyone ran from me, including my fellow Mexican-Americans. The elderly female elementary school principal rewarded me with a paddling so painful that to this day, I still remember the burning sensation each time the paddle struck my arms. That's right, my arms, not my backside. There may have been some message there, but I did not care or understand. All I know is I got the paddling of my life for trying to stop someone's hurtful words. For days afterward, no one spoke to me. I expected the Anglos to run from me, but I didn't expect my fellow Mexicans to do the same.

From that day forward, I learned not to trust anyone to come to my aid, even if they were of the same background and skin color. But that day, I also learned that standing up for bad things to stop, no matter the consequence, is worth every bit of the effort. The Anglos stopped calling me "Wetback" and "Dirty Mexican," and I became somebody not to mess with.

A couple of foreign student players from Mexico attending the local university inspired me in my tennis world. I followed the Mexican brothers in the sports page of the local paper almost daily. I figured if they played tennis and won match after match, so could I. They taught me that your will and determination to stay in the game and compete will get everyone's attention, no matter your skin color.

Many years later, I was equally proud to see two young Black women not only play tennis but win and win big. They stayed in the game, no matter that some were hostile to their being on the court. They were taunted and called ugly names but showed the world they were in it to compete and win. They got the world's attention. And I suppose that is one reason I am writing this story, to expose the truth about how C.E. and I ended up in the clutches of the angel of darkness.

Lola may not have been the warm motherly type, but she didn't abandon her children as she had been pressured to by the man who fathered me on many occasions.

I had been born from a relationship based more on sexual impulse than any type of romantic attachment. Julio Garza was an impetuous 18-year-old high school dropout, single and going nowhere when he met Lola through one of his sisters. They had nothing in common. Julio was ten years younger than Lola who had four young children from two previous marriages. It was a relationship doomed from the start.

To this day, I don't quite understand why my mother carried me to full term. It was family lore that she terminated other pregnancies, so I always wondered why she chose to bring me into the world. She paid little or no attention to her other children, so why add another to the already neglected mix? Did she use her pregnancy as leverage, so her much younger lover would marry her? Or was it because I would serve as a painful memory and nothing more from a loveless relationship doomed from the start? I suppose that's what it came down to in all manner of things. Julio never married my mother and walked away from her and me before my birth. We've met only twice and that was an awkward experience. I am more than happy that he was not a part of my life. While my mother might have been a distant and heartbreaking parent, she provided me with a shed full of survival tools to look after myself. And she supported my every whim and desire financially even after I left home. Many others around me didn't have that or any other similar support. Being raised by a single parent doesn't have to be as bad as some make it sound. Some single parents can just as easily raise a house full of children as a two-parent team. In my case, I have no doubt that, had I been raised with the type of person my father was, I wouldn't have accomplished what I did in life. I say again, thanks be to God that strange mess did not play a role in my life!

My mother was and remains one of the most fascinating figures of my life. But there was a price for living with such a person. She spent little or no time with me. I can't recall a single evening where we shared a meal together. She was not at my baptism, my first communion, my first day of school, and many significant life events. She hurt me more than any other person in my life. I can still hear one of my aunts saying under her breath: "That poor child hasn't had a bath in days. I don't think my sister cares whether Bonita lives or dies." Yet Lola could be as strict as a dictator, monitoring my every move. She confused me. One day I was ignored like an old dishrag, and the next day I was watched over as if I was a precious gem. Suffice to say, I was left to raise myself and tough it out alone.

I cannot recall whether my fifth- or sixth-grade teacher asked the class to recite assigned verses of William E. Henley's *Invictus*. My reading part from the famous poem was: "I am the master of my fate: I am the captain of my soul." Those words couldn't have come at a more propitious time, and they took hold. My young life was rudderless, driven only by pure divine guidance and true grit. I forged ahead, finding a way every day to stay focused to live in an otherwise uncaring and deadly environment. It would have been easy to step in front of one of the many vehicles speeding on our town's main street. Or to jump off the closest bridge, plunge into the warm, deep waters of the ocean and never come up. Or pretend to be asleep in one of the fields and be run over by the wheels of a trailer as many other fruit and vegetable pickers' children met their fate in nearby towns.

Being the only bastard in our family, I was more of an embarrassment than the bright, dimpled, cute, and playful child I was at heart. I often heard remarks from visitors: *"Esa es la niña?"* Their bugged-out eyes followed me as if I was some sort of circus freak. Some believed that children born out of wedlock were bad omens. They were hesitant to approach me, inching away as if my bastardly background would rub off on them. Not a good way to start life, being someone's painful memory, while a dark cloud hovered over me like—excuse me—stink on shit. There were many times when I felt no one in my family gave one dumpling whether I lived or died. Not my mother, not my half-siblings, and not even my maternal grandparents who helped raise me.

Early on, I leaned on music as my solace. No matter the type of music: jazz, classical, country, or rock-n-roll. I lost myself in the sounds made by the different instruments, and the lyrics were meaningful to me. Music soothed my soul and rescued me from the drama in my life. One time my mother, in one of her profanity-laced moods, accused me of running after boys and doing who knows what with them. Lola was free to accuse me of anything, but running after boys and having sex with them was beyond the realm of possibility. Most of the boys in my neighborhood were brother-like and the rest weren't interested in this high-octane tomboy. The neighborhood kids, made up mostly of boys, played together from morning to dusk. I beat them at marble games, shooting more birds and snakes with my BB-gun, climbing trees faster, outrunning and outpacing them on neighborhood streets. And for good measure, bashing their heads in and kicking them with my favorite Roy Rogers cowboy boots if they didn't do as I ordered. So, you tell me, who would want to date a wildcat of a girl like me? No one could tame me and no one dared try.

One day, after hearing Lola spit out enough curse words to last me a lifetime, I went to my room and turned on the radio. A song played that I had heard days earlier as the soundtrack of a movie about a circus family. It starts with: *"When life doesn't seem worth a living, and you don't really care who you are, when you feel no one beside you, look for a star."* The song kept me from running away or, worse yet, telling Lola to go to hell, which is what I desperately wanted to tell her but that would have likely cost me my life. Music saved me that day, the day after, and the day after. And decades later, when our financial life as a couple collapsed, I played Garry Miles' *'Look for a Star'* and Bill Withers' *'Lean on me'* incessantly. Like years earlier, music kept me from wrecking my life.

Yet, despite my mother's distance and callousness, she taught me much. Mostly her teachings had to do with defending myself against those who could bring me harm. Trust was her rallying cry. I can still remember the many times she told me not to trust anyone. "Hell, you can't even trust me," she bellowed repeatedly. That advice became instilled and served me well, especially living in an environment where child molestations, incest, sexual abuse, wife beatings, shootings, and knife fights were the order of the day. I dodged one dire situation after another. Decades later, my mother's words echoed in my mind as I struggled to figure out how to comfort C.E.: *"I told you not to trust anyone!"*

One day, maybe after reciting part of the poem *Invictus*, I decided to live happily, take charge of my life, direct it my way and the hell with everybody else. After all, while only a small slice, my lineage was that of knighted warriors and adventurers. The Goyos started in Grenada and later Catalonia, Spain. Their name originated from the Spanish word, *Goyo* meaning joy. And they were knighted for their warrior heroics. They may not have been the most abundant and fecund of progenitors. Still, the influence of the Goyo name is felt throughout most of the Western hemisphere. I am a part of that heritage—a proud member of the determined Jewish people who left Spain for parts unknown rather than risk being persecuted for their religious beliefs. In my case, my relatives migrated to the Nuevo Leon state of Mexico, where many Spanish Jews settled in the early days. And, like them, if I wanted to do anything with my life—anything at all—I had no choice but to leave, lest I became one more marginalized Mexican in a town filled with bigots and a shaky and unpredictable life on the town's southside. Being a warrior is part of my makeup. That nature served me well when I came to my husband's defense after he lost all means of sustaining our quality of life. I became a warrior-wife, determined to seek out the truth.

I was the first in my family to graduate from high school, and I was the first to leave home, but with a suitcase filled with notebooks, calculator, pens, pencils, and clothes. But not with a spouse like my siblings did years earlier. I had a plan to create something different—better—than what I'd seen some family members do with their lives. It was time to not only leave the family but also the forsaken racist hometown I was born and raised in, a place where I felt my life would amount to not much of anything.

I moved in with a cousin who lived in a city much larger than my hometown to attend secretarial school. My mother had saved enough money to send me to a four-year college, but I was afraid that my high school study habits and socializing would carry on to college. I didn't want to be known as the first in my family to go to college and the first one in town to be sent home for attending one party too many. So, I took the easy way out and decided to learn to be a secretary and figure my real career later. When I told Lola what I intended to do, she didn't argue with me as she was known to do constantly. She hopped in her shiny red Buick Skylark, with the car radio blasting all kinds of Spanish songs as she drove me to my cousin's home 100 miles away at record speed while knocking back a couple of beers. I swear that woman smoked one Camel cigarette after another like there was no tomorrow, while passing cars as if she was being chased by the police. I was all too happy to climb out of the red Skylark and into my cousin's warm and lovely home. After a few bits of advice from Lola, mainly don'ts, she jumped back into her still running car. I eagerly waved Lola good-bye and turned the page to a new chapter in my life. Once I moved in with my cousin, I took control of my life much as I would in New York city, where I moved two years later and Washington, D.C where I ended up. I no longer had Lola breathing down my neck. I was free to make my own choices in life and own them, which I have ever since.

Everything C.E. lost, I lost too: dignity, self-respect, even—at the lowest point—my will to live. When C.E. lost his company and his job and all prospects for what we both believed was a prosperous and promising future, that spirit of strength and toughness—the positive attributes I received from my mother—left me. I felt devoid of hope, my soul empty. I was no longer the master of my fate and the captain of my soul. Instead, I found myself on my knees, sobbing and wishing for redemption, while ignoring any kind of spiritual guidance. I was—I thought at the time—an irreparably broken spirit, crying and carrying on like someone I did not recognize. I became a stranger to myself. Where were my Goyo ancestors and my warrior lineage when I needed them the most?

I became collateral damage from a situation not of my own choosing or my own doing. I had everything one day and nothing the next. I knew how Ruth Madoff must have felt when her husband lost all their wealth. But her situation was the obverse of mine. Her husband, Bernie Madoff, lost everything because he cheated others, while my husband lost everything because others he trusted cheated him.

As soon as C.E.'s six-figure paycheck stopped, everything that could go bad did. Our credit rating sank to rock bottom, and the bills piling up on my desk frightened me and constantly reminded me of our financial demise. With our bad credit, we quickly learned neither of us could find jobs at a level commensurate with our professional experience and academic credentials. We were unemployable. Our financial life became so desperate that I even thought of applying for a job at McDonald's, but I understood they too had a vetting process. About a year after C.E. lost his job, I heard from an old friend out of the blue that had once helped the federal agency I headed many years earlier. He ran a nonprofit organization and called to ask if I was interested in helping with their humanitarian effort. It had been over twenty years since I had last heard from him.

I believe God puts angels in our paths to help navigate our lives. And when my old contact called me, I felt God's hand upon me. My hiring came when money was desperately needed to keep C.E. and me from becoming homeless. Our country home—our only residence—was about to be foreclosed, too. That's how bad things got for us. I was hired because of my expertise in the subject of humanitarian aid to refugees and migrants. But I also felt that, had I not treated the director of the nonprofit and his staff with respect and kindness when they helped our agency, he may not have hired me, no matter my experience. The words 'you reap what you sow' have meaning to us all. It's not so much what you know but how you treat people that stays in people's minds, and that alone can sink you or float opportunities you would not otherwise have been presented.

I ended up working for my friend's non-profit for five years. During that time, I was able help pay down our debt and start living again. But, like all things that look good at first, there was more to the organization than met the eye. After many years of providing services to the federal government, some of the nonprofit's executive staff, including its director, my friend, became embroiled in a federal funding controversy that cost them their jobs.

It was sad and disappointing to see my friend retiring from the successful organization he had built for over thirty years. Even though I didn't get paid anywhere commensurate with my experience, I was grateful to earn what I could to make our financial lives easier. Then the new leaders of the organization decided to not extend my contract when it expired, though there remained much work to be done in their humanitarian effort. Almost everyone the former director had hired was tainted, and

I took a hit. Once again, I became collateral damage, two words that were becoming to define me.

As luck would have it, about a week after my contract expired with my friend's non-profit, a friend called urging me to apply for a senior level consultant position with a major corporation. I took her advice, mailed in my resume to the company's president and CEO. His assistant called almost immediately for an interview. Before I had time to bleach my ever-growing gray hair, I found myself in front of the CEO and his senior managers. They fired questions from every direction. It reminded me of the interview I had with a cast of about ten people for a federal post almost thirty years earlier. The deputy of the federal department showed up with his management team, firing questions about an array of issues ranging from politics to where I was born. I sat on a leather Gibson-style sofa surrounded by the deputy and his team, one of whom became a popular television commentator. I figured if I survived and was hired after being interviewed by that group of aggressive interviewers, surely I could handle the CEO and his team of mostly retired military flag officers.

After my interview, I was immediately hired as Senior Advisor to the president and CEO of the company. I could not believe my timing and my luck. Since C.E. lost his job and company, good fortune seemed to run the other way. Even though I had found work with my friend's non-profit, their pay was barely enough to get us by. This was different. The company's compensation offer was more than I expected. It was enough to regain my confidence and get our financial life back.

Every morning I wake up, I thank God for his blessings and make it a point not to spend one more minute looking back at what happened to C.E., which also happened to me. I fear that keeping my eye on those dark days may well turn me into a pillar of salt like Lot's wife as she left Sodom and Gomorrah.

Chapter 6

I Should Have Been a Lawyer

"Lawyers spend a great deal of their time
shoveling smoke."
—Oliver Wendell Holmes, Jr.

"Why are you here?" the judge asked C.E.'s lawyer.

Her abrupt and hostile question kicked my heart down to my knees. "What the shit was all that about?" I whispered to C.E.

"Bad day at the office," C.E. responded solemnly.

The mild-looking lawyer representing C.E. seemed to morph down to pint-sized. His face turned beet red, and I was sure he would keel over. Shifting from one foot to the other while saying nothing to explain why his case was in the judge's court, the lawyer made no reference to the critical issues of C.E.'s case. Instead, he nervously muttered that C.E.—once a well-to-do man—was about to lose one of his homes.

The judge raised her head from a document on her desk. Her eyes lasered on the man. I imagined her saying or thinking: *One of his homes! Who the hell cares about the general's second home? I barely own one, and if all I am going to hear is about this man losing a second home, you jerk, you just lost your client's case.*

A dreadful thought came to me, *C.E.'s case was dead on arrival*!

The lawyer C.E. hired had come highly recommended by a former business associate of C.E.'s. The man was the same person that met C.E. years earlier when he was the lead investigator into the wrongdoings of a company that C.E. once served on the board of. From the start, C.E. wasn't too keen on suing either his former company, C.E. Inc., or Green and Steele's, C.E. LLC. He wanted to put his company's asset sale nightmare behind him. But I convinced him otherwise: "Something doesn't smell right, Levy. You ought to find a lawyer to take your case *pro bono*. I think a good lawyer should be able to get back the two-year severance that your former company owes you. You can also go after C.E. LLC for having canceled your consulting agreement before you had the chance to attend the corporate board's first meeting."

I admit that was naïve on my part since, at the time, I didn't fully understand all the nuances associated with the asset sale and C.E.'s lawyer's intentions to take his case.

So, we began our crusade. But every lawyer we met or spoke with was reluctant to take C.E.'s case. "You signed and signed and signed… it's all one document too many." One lawyer after another repeated the exact words.

But I did not want to give in that easily: "Oh, what do they know? Let's think this through. Who do we know has the *cojones* to take this case on?"

C.E., in his usual soft-spoken way, said he was thinking of contacting the person who helped with the investigation of the former company he had been associated with to help him find a lawyer. "He was the lawyer that helped investigate the wrongdoings by the company's executive team. And he did a pretty damn good job. I trust him."

My fingers hit the computer's keyboard and searched before C.E. finished his sentence. "Here he is!" I yelled excitedly.

C.E. wanted to wait and think about it.

"What in the world are you waiting for?" I questioned. "We are about to lose our asses, and you want to wait. Wait for what? For you to win the lottery? For a miracle to happen? Let's get this fucking show on the road. Call him up, or I will."

His former business associate responded to C.E.'s message before the end of the day. They scheduled a luncheon at a busy restaurant but chose a quiet table to discuss C.E.'s concerns. I joined them after their meeting. It was clear that the former investigator and lawyer admired and liked C.E. and wanted to help him. "If it quacks like a duck and walks like a duck, it is a duck," he said assuredly, following us out of the club. "I'll send you the names of several lawyers that might want to help you."

We received his list and started calling them. All said the same thing the attorneys we contacted previously had: "You've signed one document too many, general. Sorry. Don't think I can help you." The list was down to one name.

"Who's left?" C.E. asked anxiously.

"Some fellow that your old contact said is a close friend.

"Well, what do you think?" C.E. asked. "Should we call him or call it quits?"

"Let's cross ourselves and say a Hail Mary," I answered.

Two days later, we met with a reserved, Hispanic-looking man in his late fifties. He was courteous and seemed eager to hear C.E.'s case, especially since his old friend had referred us to him. His close to thirty-five years of experience practicing law was impressive. Nothing during our meeting raised any concerns about him, personal or otherwise.

Roberto Fitzpatrick proudly pointed to his names which came from his Spanish and Irish ancestors before announcing that he would take C.E.'s case. "We have zero money," I told him up front, and he assured C.E. would be charged according to his and his assistant's hourly fees on a pay-as-you-go basis. "It's a sort of credit card type deal," he explained, "and you pay what you can afford." But he stressed that all out-of-pocket expenses were to be paid as soon as they were billed. "They won't be much," he assured us.

We walked out of the lawyer's office convinced justice was around the corner for the first time since C.E. lost his job about six months earlier. We felt that this lawyer was the man who could collect C.E.'s severance from his former company and consulting agreement monies from C.E. LLC. He seemed determined to get what was owed C.E. Our second meeting with our newly hired lawyer was promptly scheduled. He asked for full disclosure of C.E.'s recollection that led to him losing C.E. Inc. and how C.E. LLC came to be formed and ended up with the entire company for a mere $3.4 million.

C.E. did his best to answer all the lawyer's questions before breaking down. But the more questions he asked, the sillier they got. He even asked what Charlie Kaka was wearing the day he told C.E. he was kicked off C.E. LLC's board. We became concerned about his handling of C.E.'s case, but he held up hope since he was the only one willing to take it on.

C.E. kept bringing his now-hired lawyer back to the issue at hand. "The bank was responsible for C.E. Inc.'s assets to be sold for the low and insulting price of $3.4 million," he stressed. "Let's go after the bank," C.E. urged.

Roberto waved him off: "I'm not going after a bank that has a ton of lawyers to defend it. I'll concentrate on C.E. LLC and your former company."

Midway through that meeting, the law firm's principal partner and co-founder joined us. After the usual handshake greetings, the heavy-set gentleman assured us that Roberto Fitzpatrick was the man to help C.E. He would be the lead lawyer in C.E.'s case, while he, the principal partner, would be involved only remotely, if at all. He confessed that he had a past association with the bank that was C.E. Inc.'s lender, but assured us he was no longer actively involved. "Don't worry about that," he said. "I will not be involved in your case anyway. Besides, I'm not too happy with the way the bank does some of their business."

The only thing on our minds was finding someone to take C.E.'s case. We let go of our concern about his lawyer's decision to eliminate the bank in the lawsuit. We believed there was a case against both companies. And we thought Fitzpatrick and his law firm did too, or why take on a case that has no merit? But as soon as we walked out of the law firm's office, I turned to C.E. and said: "I don't know, something's not right with the law firm's lead partner being a former associate of the bank. Remember, for every law firm we called, the first thing they asked was the names of the parties involved in your suit, to make sure they didn't have any ties to the bank or either of the two companies that would be a conflict of interest." The more I thought about it, the more likely the firm's founder's association with the bank could be a problem for us. I cautioned C.E. as we rode the elevator down to the building's lobby. "Do you think this law firm can help you without including the bank"? I have a bad feeling about this," C.E. agreed. But C. E. was in desperate need of a lawyer.

During my time in graduate school, all two hundred or so of the school's student enrollment could cross-register at any of the university's professional schools. I registered to take a basic course at the university's law school. Since the day my sister's husband went to a state prison for having two marijuana cigarettes in his coat pocket, the law had intrigued me. When the lawyer whom my mother hired and paid a hefty advancement to defend my brother-in-law didn't show up during my brother-in-law's court hearing and sentencing, I thought, *Who pulls that kind of shit*? And so, my sister's husband, through inadequate legal representation, ended up in jail far longer than others that committed more serious crimes. For years, that event stuck in my mind, which prompted me to take that introductory law course, thinking that if I liked law enough, I would become a lawyer one day to save those unjustly tried and inadequately served.

Not that I cared what happened to my brother-in-law. He was an uncaring husband to my sister and an even worse father to their five children. Parading about town chasing every woman he could find, dressed in the finest clothes while my sister and her children wore hand-me-downs. But he deserved justice. And he was one brother-in-law who didn't try to molest me. Can't say the same for one other brother-in-law, who constantly preyed on me. I was a regular babysitter for my sister and her husband's two children. Those times were spent mostly fending off my brother-in-law's advances. During the one and only school vacation that I agreed to babysit their children for the entire summer, I found myself on my first day of work thrown against the bed while my brother-in-law held me down forcefully, working to pull down my panties until I smacked his face so hard it drew blood from his nose and mouth. After that, he left me alone but only for a while. The advances continued.

I figured with the type of aggressive behavior my sister's husband displayed toward me day after day, my luck would run out and I'd end up losing my virginity and worse yet, become pregnant, which was very likely since the women in my family were known to be big time breeders. My sisters and our mother Lola would joke that all a man had to do was look at them and they'd become pregnant. My sister's husband had made previous advances, but I was better positioned to walk away. This time I was literally at his mercy. When he arrived for lunch every day, we'd play cat and mouse. I'd run away from him going from room to room so he wouldn't catch up with me. Then I'd grab both children and carry them outside and remained there until he drove off. One day, he left and returned almost immediately, surprising me while I was preparing the children for their afternoon naps. He grabbed me from behind and dragged me into the master bedroom. I was frightened out of my wits, and I didn't scare easily. While I fought him off, the children saved me when they followed us into the room.

I had never loved the month of September more, when school finally started, which I credit for saving my innocence. In the way of my family, a girl didn't complain about such happenings as I experienced with my brother-in-law. If you did, you'd be accused of having invited such attention. My family's antiquated thinking and unusual cultural beliefs helped to get me to recognize that I had no choice but to jump out of the family circle as soon as I could lest I started thinking like them.

The law class I took was boring. Yet I was convinced that I could have made a damn good lawyer, in the likeness of my favorite lawyer Richard "Racehorse" Haynes. He was a criminal defense attorney who became a star of the legal world after winning a series of impossible murder trials. His legal preparation including sizing up the jury, dressing up his clients, and tearing apart the opposition. He was my kind of lawyer, and I wanted someone like him to represent C.E.'s lawsuit. But with our empty pockets, that was not going to happen.

As it turned out, C.E.'s attorney didn't measure up to the famous lawyer, not even close. C.E. and I continued our conversation about his shortcomings. "I knew I should have applied to law school when I had the chance," I told C.E. "We've been desperately trying to find a lawyer to take your case. We find one, only to learn the law firm is associated with the very bank that screwed you. Have we both taken leave of our senses or what?" I shook my head.

"It doesn't do any good to look back, Bonita. We are where we are, and I accept my share of the blame for that," C.E. said quietly.

"Please, don't repeat those words again," I cried out. "Remember, it wasn't you that decided to only sell C.E. Inc's assets. Just give me time. I'll have it figured out before you know it," I said assuredly.

At the time neither of us were aware that C.E. LCC had taken C.E. Inc's federally-assigned proprietary number. Nor did we know that the Final Contract Sale Agreement was being introduced by C.E. LLC as a document that C.E. signed, which he had not.

The more we met with C.E's lawyer, the crazier it got. He had us donning triangle-shaped paper hats on our heads to rehearse our day in court. In one practice session, he turned to me and ordered: "Tell the court your name."

"Aaaah, Bonita Levine," I answered timidly.

"You want to speak up. Let the court hear you. You'll need to practice more so you aren't nervous when you testify," he demanded, then added sternly, "And, Bonita, you want to change your wardrobe. You look like a rich lady, and the court won't like that when you testify."

"What a bunch of cockamamie bullshit," I blurted out as soon the doors closed behind us. "C.E., did you hear what he said? 'You look like a rich lady,'" I tried to mimic the lawyer's voice. "What does that have to do with the price of gasoline in a civil courtroom?" As we entered the elevator, I continued, "Let me tell you something else. All this rehearsing the lawyer is doing with us is a way for him to rack up hours to charge you. Hell, you haven't had your first hearing in front of a judge, and he's acting as if there will be a jury trial. I'm telling you, Levy, this is nothing more than pure chicken-shit made up to give you false hope that you will get the chance to plead your case before a jury. I am beginning to think that your lawyer is leading you down a primrose lane to throw you off from pursuing the real culprit in all of this, the bank, and charge you a ton of money in the process."

I don't know who the bigger fools were, C.E.'s lawyer for putting us through the silly charade or me and C.E. for being so desperate for legal representation we were willing to subject ourselves to such money-wasting nonsense. All I could think of was, *I now know I should have been a lawyer.*

C.E. never pleaded his case or anything else before a jury. The law firm representing C.E. LLC filed for a summary judgment, and the judge accepted it. C.E.'s lawyer didn't know whether to shit or wind his watch during the hearing. His over-the-top nervousness and beet-red sweaty face made me think he was hiding something. In my opinion, his behavior and nervousness that day were most likely the result of guilt for telling the court that C.E. had not read the Contract Sale Agreement or because he planned it that way to help the opposition. He had little to offer in C.E.'s defense for all his posturing and talk. Yet the judge, known as a demanding and hard-nosed judge, made two helpful rulings. She ordered Roberto to file a judgment against C.E. Inc. for his severance and ordered that C.E. LLC owed C.E. their initial consulting agreement offer of $100,000. While she was sympathetic to C.E.'s plight, she admonished him for signing one document too many with C.E. LLC and not hiring a lawyer in the process. She ended by saying to Roberto that he should have gone after the bank because they were the ones that started all this.

Mistakes were made in thinking that Roberto had C.E.'s best interest. Why wouldn't C.E. think that the lawyer who was charging enormous fees was putting all his talent and resources to help C.E.? No doubt C.E. should have fired Roberto the minute after he told the court that C.E. had not read the Contract Sale Agreement. But during the entire time we met with Roberto, he emphasized that C.E. need not worry about the Contract Sale Agreement because he could get around it. During that time, C.E. thought his lawyer was referring to the contract sale agreement framework that he acknowledged he signed and showed to his lawyer the first day we both met with him. It would be years later after the court hearing that C.E. discovered the Contract Sale Agreement presented in court was not the framework document he showed his lawyer initially but rather it was the Final Version of the Contract Sale Agreement, a document he hadn't seen, much less signed.

C.E.'s lawyer filed a judgment against C.E. Inc. for his severance totaling almost $1.3 million, but only after being ordered by the judge to do so. But a court magistrate ruled that C.E. could not receive his severance because he didn't have a separation agreement from C.E. Inc. The court ruled that C.E. could only receive $42,000 for his days as an employee of his former company, and half of that total would go to his counsel. Shouldn't C.E.'s lawyer have seen this coming? All he had to do was follow the paper trail and listen to C.E., who told him he had not signed a separation agreement from his C.E. Inc. because Sean Sneek advised that he didn't need one.

When we walked out of the courtroom, I turned to C.E. "That's one hell of a ruling. But think about this. If the court has ruled that you don't have a separation agreement, you must still be tied to your former company. Remember what Dick Small, the lawyer representing C.E. LLC, answered when the judge asked him if C.E. Inc. had been dissolved? Small said it had not been. Damn it, I wish the judge had asked him that if your company is not dissolved, then who is running it? Your lawyer should have asked that question. Instead, he said nothing and stood in the courtroom looking like a defeated wrestler, soaked in his own sweat. I am not liking this one bit, C.E."

C.E.'s case could have taken a turn to his advantage had his lawyer asked the right question. According to all the players involved in the asset sale and the Final Contract Sale Agreement, C.E. Inc. was to be dissolved within ten days after the asset sale. A year later, the company was still alive. C.E. LLC didn't buy the entity, so they had no right to it. So, who was running C.E. Inc.? Who had the responsibility to dissolve it?

As we continued to our car, I turned to C.E. and said excitedly: "Listen, I have a feeling that C.E. LLC is actively playing in C.E. Inc.'s playground. Your lawyer ought to read C.E. LLC's lawyers the riot act. He has the leverage to do that, don't you think? Maybe your lawyer can work on C.E. LLC to help separate you from your former company, which they are apparently controlling, and get you your severance. While at the same time, tie up all the loose ends that the lender and you and the buyers left hanging."

Little did I know at the time just how complex and convoluted the asset sale of C.E. Inc.'s asset sale was, from start to finish.

"Okay, Bonita," C.E. agreed, "let's allow my lawyer to show he has the balls to ask C.E. LLC the right questions." We both laughed—one of the few times in those days—as we got in our car.

But C.E.'s lawyer ran from our idea like a frightened husband after being caught in a cheap motel with his lover. Yet the court's ruling was a blessing in disguise. It triggered that part of me that knew I would have been not just a lawyer but a damn good one. I went into research mode to find out who was running C.E. Inc., since Small had said it was still in existence. Was there money running through it? How much? Who collected that money? And remember, C.E.'s former production chief told me that C.E. LLC had diverted shipment monies due them back into C.E. Inc. I made it my mission to get to the bottom of it all. Where there's smoke, there's fire! Or, as C.E.'s old contact said: "If it quacks like a duck and walks like a duck, it's a duck."

Roberto didn't collect the monies awarded to C.E. by the court from either his C.E. Inc. or from C.E. LLC. Instead, he pushed to appeal the court's ruling against C.E. He worked hard to convince C.E. that he could get the judge's decision turned around.

"On what basis?" we both asked in unison.

He reassured us: "I can't promise you that all three appeals judges will agree with us. But all it takes is one judge to rule in our favor. I have to tell you, if you folks want to go forward, I'll have to get paid for the appeal and for all you owe the firm for the past several months."

C.E. and I didn't have the funds to pay him. He had racked up his charges to well over six figures in less than a year.

"We don't have one penny to continue. Hell, we don't even know how we are going to pay for the work you've done," C.E. anxiously replied.

"Don't worry about it," he reassured us, "we can work something out. I believe your case stands a good chance of being turned around."

C.E. and I glanced at one another. Our eyes rolled upward as if to say, *"Let's bolt this joint."* We wanted more than anything to get what we thought C.E. was due. But seeing as we were already up to our eyeballs in debt with the law firm, we didn't want to get in deeper. We stood up to gather our things and shake Roberto's hand to thank him for his work when he began waving his hands for us to return to our seats.

"I have an idea," he said as if a lighted bulb suddenly appeared over his head. He came up with a payment method we didn't like that had to do with essentially taking partial possession of one of our homes, but we were both desperate, and desperation can turn even the most thoughtful thinkers into fools. We had many questions and concerns, but the lawyer's offer dangled before us like the promise of a winning lottery ticket. I had every reason to be reluctant to take the lawyer's offer. C.E. had been taken to the cleaners, and we were still suffering the consequences. Yet I knew how much it meant to C.E. to get what was owed to him by C.E. LLC, which was the center of his case in the appeals process. We took his offer. But we should have stopped his work and walked away with a lesser debt than the amount C.E. ended up owing.

The appeals hearing was a total disaster. All three of the judges ruled almost immediately against C.E., although before their decision, one judge asked the law firm's associate attorney serving as counsel in Roberto's stead if C.E. could prove he had been on the board of directors of the C.E. LLC. And he could. As proof that C.E. was a member of C.E. LLC's board of directors, the trio of Green, Steele, and Kaka, along with C.E., signed documents saying all four acknowledged the Final Contract Sale Agreement. C.E. did not have a copy of this document. But the associate attorney substituting for Roberto had one in her possession and had shared it with both of us a few days before the appeals hearing.

C.E. and I felt a flare of hope. Might this be the break we needed to get someone to look at the facts and evidence?

But the associate counsel stared off into space and didn't offer a response to the judge. It was as if someone had coached her to say nothing or not provide any documentation supporting C.E.'s case. C.E. and I both wanted to jump out of our chairs to holler out the answer. But we both remembered that Roberto told us a few days earlier that the appeals court hearing rules didn't allow C.E. to speak—only his legal counsel could.

In my opinion, the associate counsel could have helped C.E.'s case during the appeal hearing. She could have presented to the judge the same board document she had shown C.E. and me days earlier that proved he had been a member of C.E. LLC's board. But if she had, the document would reveal the truth behind C.E.'s signature in the board document acknowledging the Final Contract Sale Agreement, which C.E. had not seen at that time of the remote board meeting. The omission of this critical evidence may have had a completely different outcome to C.E.'s case.

Roberto Fitzpatrick didn't show up for C.E.'s appeal hearing, just like the lawyer representing my sister's husband didn't show up almost fifty-five years earlier. In the case of my brother-in-law, he was an under-educated member of the lower income ranks of American society. That wasn't so with C.E. yet C.E. and my brother-in-law were both victims of the legal system.

Soon after the appeals hearing, C.E.'s lawyer sent a letter to C.E. telling him the law firm had concluded its engagement with him. The lawyer further said he would not pursue collecting the court's ruling award to C.E. He added that C.E.'s outstanding bill was in mid-six figures and growing due to interest fees.

It took us almost four years, without any legal assistance, to determine how C.E. LLC ended up with all C.E.'s Inc.'s contracts without a federally-assigned proprietary number of its own and without novating or subcontracting them from C.E. Inc. And it took almost that same amount of time to come to realize that he should never have hired Roberto Fitzpatrick. C.E. thought of filing a lawsuit against the law firm at one point. But he quickly learned that hiring a law firm to file a lawsuit against another law firm from the same state is nearly impossible. And there is a statute of limitations to contend with. A word of caution: suing a law firm is one of the most challenging legal processes. The law firms know that, and I suspect they don't lose much sleep worried about legal action against them.

A few months after C.E. Inc.'s asset sale, Pancho O'Grady excitedly called C.E. He told him that the C.E. LLC had sold itself to a much bigger company for about $50 million, close to the exact figure of the pending contracts C.E. Inc. had been pre-awarded before the asset sale. "We didn't do bad! Those are our contracts the motherfuckers stole and sold, or should I say resold. They didn't invent any new products or win any new contracts; it was all our contracts that were pre-awarded prior to the asset sale and fully funded after the asset sale. They stole them in clear daylight. You were right all along C.E. We should have never signed the contract sale agreement framework. It was a nothing document and the bank couldn't have forced us to sign it."

After C.E. hung up with Pancho, he was not exactly jumping up and down. I walked over to him and wrapped my arms around him and advised: "You may want to write to the new owners of C.E. LLC and tell them about the court's ruling that you don't have a separation agreement from C.E. Inc. It sure as hell sounds to me that your former company continues to be alive, and C.E. LLC seems to be the one controlling it. Besides, you and I both know that C.E. LLC didn't pay for your company's pending contracts, which they ended up with and resold.

C.E. turned around and said firmly, "Bonita, you may be right, but I am getting awfully tired of all of this. These fucking people are so damn crooked they make Bonnie and Clyde look honest and that's what I am up against, fucking professional crooks."

"Well, at least go on record as having warned the Midwest company. Let them know you know what went on and continues to go on," I advised.

C.E. nodded. "Okay, I'll write the letter, and you can edit it since you know more about what went on with the asset sale."

The letter was mailed to the president and CEO of the Midwest company and to the chairman of the company's board of directors. They didn't respond. C.E. sent a second letter reiterating to both men that he did not have a separation agreement and was pursuing a lawsuit against their newly bought company. He told them the $30 million contract was fraudulently awarded to C.E. LLC, which meant the company didn't rightfully own that contract and had no authority to sell it to their company. The Midwest company responded by hiring Horace Steele as a Senior Vice President.

Shortly after C.E. mailed the second letter to the Midwest firm, C.E., Pancho and I and a friend from Colorado well-versed in white collar corruption revived C.E. Inc. The Colorado friend advised C.E. and Pancho that anyone could restore the corporation. They needed to pay the back corporate taxes and file reinstatement paperwork with the state's tax office. That advice was seconded by the staff of the state's tax department.

C.E. revived C.E. Inc. because he did not have a separation agreement from his former company, and was concerned how he was affected, legally or otherwise. He set out to learn about anything C.E. Inc. under C.E. LLC's control had done or was doing that would negatively impact him. But no sooner was the ink dry on C.E.'s signature that the law firm that represented C.E. LLC sent a letter to C.E. stating that C.E. had no right to revive his former company, referencing the Final Contract Sale Agreement that stated that C.E. LLC owned the name of his former company forever, meaning that two companies with the same name couldn't exist. This was news to C.E. He had not seen the Final Contract Sale Agreement at the time and wasn't familiar with such a policy. C.E. dug in his heels instead of complying with the law firm to dissolve C.E. Inc. He thought the law firm acted too quickly to keep him from reviving his former company. What did they think he was going to do with the company? What did they think he was going to learn about its operations under their client's control? So, he once again asked the bank for a copy of the so-called Final Contract Sale Agreement.

For almost four years after the asset sale, we heard little from Pancho O'Grady. But after his call with Pancho about C.E. LLC selling itself to the Midwest company, C.E. continued to answer Pancho's calls, but reluctantly. He didn't want any reminders of their life at C.E. Inc. It was too painful for C.E. to look back at what might have been, But I felt Pancho knew what really transpired in the days right before, but especially after the sale of C.E. Inc.'s assets, which could be good to know and encouraged C.E. to continue talking with him.

It turned out that Pancho had plenty of information unknown to C.E. about the behavior of the bank, Sean Sneek, Simon Green, Horace Steele, Charlie Kaka, Archer Knave, and Judith Wurm leading up to and after the sale of C.E. Inc.'s assets. He was free to talk since he didn't sign a non-disclosure agreement with C.E. LLC. He recalled that Gustavo Feo, the day after the asset sale, came into his office and asked him how the product shipments worked in terms of becoming actual income. Pancho explained to C.E. and me that, at the time, he couldn't understand why Feo asked such a question. Never in a million years did he think they would interfere with the product shipment dates, which could be legally questionable. Ultimately, Pancho focused on the $30 million federal contract that he and C.E. had pre-won, concluding that they ought to contact the government agency in charge of the contract that C.E. LLC claimed had been awarded to them. Pancho thought that, by alerting the agency they had fraudulently awarded a multi-million-dollar contract to C.E. LLC, the agency and the new owners of C.E. LLC would want to help fix the issue. C.E. agreed that the contract should not have been awarded to C.E. LLC for a variety of reasons. There was plenty to raise with the agency: how C.E. LLC ended up with the enormous contract that they didn't novate or subcontract with C.E. Inc., how they never submitted a proposal for the said contract, and many other questions. C.E. and Pancho's opinion was it would be a simple fix to get the contract aligned with the federal acquisition regulations.

In a perfect legal world, the agency would allow C.E. to novate the multi-million-dollar contract to C.E. LLC or subcontract to C.E. Inc. After all, C.E. Inc. was still in existence, and C.E. was not separated from the company. But did Green and Steele really want this help?

C.E. and Pancho 's letter to the agency's director explained that the agency had mis-awarded the contract to C.E. LLC because it had not submitted a proposal for the contract. But because at that time C.E. was not fully aware that C.E. LLC had ended up with C.E. Inc's federally-assigned proprietary number, this critical point was left out of the letter, which, if revealed, might have had a more devastating effect on the C.E. LLC and might have possibly led to a different outcome for the financial lives of ourselves and other people. C.E. and Pancho requested that the director assign someone at the senior level to investigate the contract's process from beginning to end. The letter was copied to the three heads of the Midwest company, the board chair, the CEO, and its new president.

A few days later, the law firm representing C.E. LLC wrote a scathing letter to the agency director refuting everything C.E. and Pancho addressed in their letter. The law firm's letter explained why their client ended up with the multi-million-dollar contract, referring to the Final Contract Sale Agreement, which stated all future contracts were part of the asset sale. This was not a document that C.E. nor his two officers had signed. But because C.E.'s lawyer failed to address this fact in court, the judge ruled the document was legitimate. Because of this, C.E. could never reopen that aspect of the case in any civil court. But the law firm didn't stop there. They had to get into the dirt. The lawyer writing the letter, Dick Small called C.E. all kinds of insulting and degrading names and even questioned his rank and honor. Who was Dick Small to cite the standards expected of General Officers? He served in the Air Force for a very short period and certainly not as a flag officer. While he was casting stones at a highly-decorated soldier, Small should have looked at his own behavior and the law firm he represented. C.E.'s letter to the agency director implied that the $30 million contract was fraudulently awarded. But, in their response to C.E.'s charges in the letter, C.E. LLC's law firm, rather than defend it in its proper legal form, chose to disparage C.E. in a most unprofessional and disrespectful manner, unbecoming of a law firm. But that was not surprising. This law firm was ruthless in its representation of C.E. LLC against C.E. Everything that the law firm cited in its letter related to the Final Contract Sale Agreement, a document that C.E. and his two officers did not sign. But C.E.'s lawyer, rather than question the document's validity, allowed the law firm to introduce the fraudulent document against his own client in court. Or did C.E.'s lawyer know the truth behind the signed pages, as well as C.E. LLC's lawyers? Who did know how those signed pages got in that document in the first place? I'll give you one guess.

During the lawsuit, Roberto informed C.E. that he met with C.E. LLC's other assigned lawyer on several occasions. Before C.E. could ask why, the lawyer rushed to explain: "I know the lawyer, he's a good guy. Opposing lawyers always try to meet to ease tensions between the plaintiff and the defendant."

C.E. never approved such meetings, yet his lawyer charged him hundreds of dollars to meet with the opposition's lawyer. The moral of the story: When hiring a lawyer, you have every right to tell the lawyer what you expect. If the lawyer doesn't listen to you, find another lawyer, which is what C.E., in retrospect, should have done.

A few days after C.E. LLC's lawyers sent their letter to the agency director, Pancho wrote a letter to both the law firm and to the agency director denying he was an active board member of C.E. Inc., adding that he never intended to write the letter. C.E. was caught blind-sided. He didn't receive a copy of Pancho's letter until well after the law firm and the agency received theirs. The law firm quickly used the letter to defend their client against C.E.'s. and Pancho's charges. C.E. was understandably disappointed in Pancho's action, but I was livid, ready to read him the riot act and, while I was at it, beat the living shit out of him. But C.E. reasoned that Pancho likely got scared from being sued. He wasn't wrong— C.E. got sued almost immediately thereafter. I never forgave Pancho but, at the same time, I couldn't blame him. He stood to lose a lot more than we had. Hiring lawyers to defend you is costly, plus the legal process can stress you into an early grave.

C.E. wrote a second letter to the agency director, reemphasizing his concerns about the award of the multi-million-dollar contract to the C.E LLC. This time, though, he took it a step further and declared himself an official whistleblower. The agency director never responded to either of C.E.'s letters, nor acknowledged his whistleblower declaration, which federal law required him to do.

Shortly after C.E. sent his second letter, two different law firms representing C.E. LLC filed a restraining order against C.E. to keep him from further contacting the federal agency about the multi-million-dollar contract or any of C.E. LLC's contracts with any government agency. It so happened that the week C.E. received the restraining order, a close friend from California Maria Perez-Delaney was visiting us. When Maria learned that C.E. was planning to represent himself at the hearing, she went ballistic. "They'll chop you up in pieces. You can't go alone."

C.E. answered, "I wish I didn't have to, but I can't afford a lawyer."

Those two words—"can't afford"—were now frequently used by C.E., but that did not make them any less bitter to say. Later that day, Maria volunteered to call someone she knew with a private law practice. Not long after that call, C.E, my friend, and I were on the phone with her West Coast lawyer friend, who seemed eager to help C.E. on a pro bono basis. But the problem was there were limitations to how much she could assist. Yet, somehow, the temporary restraining order was delayed.

A few days later after our call with my friend's lawyer, the two firms filed a complaint against C.E. for thousands of dollars because he alerted the agency director about the multi-million-dollar contract. The civil complaint accused C.E. of everything they could put in a kitchen sink and then some. A principal in the secondary law firm, ordered C.E.—an 83-year-old man with no money and no legal representation who suffered from stress-related health issues due to the asset sale fallout—to comply with the order. Was this necessary? Or was he trying to bully C.E.?

C.E. LLC hired a third law firm. Its lead attorney wrote a letter to the agency director, telling him that C.E. LLC, through their new owner, the Midwest company, retained the law firm to represent them concerning alleged violations of the federal acquisition regulations and procurement fraud raised by C.E. The attorney further stated that they were specifically retained to investigate the facts and circumstances of the contract award and would provide a legal opinion on whether any procurement fraud was present. Interestingly, the copy of the law firm's letter provided to C.E. by C.E. LLC was not signed. In C.E.'s opinion, it was another smoke and mirror on the part of C.E. LLC to scare him off. He never received a copy of the law firm's legal opinion of the contract in question.

This is what law firms do on behalf of their clients (and to defend themselves). They take no prisoners. In another instance, C.E. LLC's primary law firm took up for the bank, stating that the bank was tired of lending money to C.E. Inc. What bank, especially one with millions in profit, would be "tired" of lending money? Did they think they could convince anyone that the bank was being drained by a small company that paid high interest rates on its loan for several years, had close to $50 million in upcoming federal contracts, and was valued at between $30-35 million? And if it was so tired, why did the bank allow C.E. LLC to pay only half of the loan that C.E. Inc. owed them and not the entire amount? The law firm, at one point, even said that C.E. well knew what was in the Final Contract Sale Agreement since he was shown bits and pieces of the document throughout the asset sale process. Are we in outer space here or what? Bits and pieces do not constitute C.E. reviewing, approving, and signing the entire Final Contract Sale Agreement. But C.E.'s lawyer didn't argue against such reasoning. Throw all the shit they can muster against you and try to get some of it to stick. Unless the defendant has a savvy lawyer, they are in for a big loss.

C.E. waited to hear a reply from the agency director or an investigator about the agency's multi-million-dollar contract. But, during this time, the new legal advisor called C.E. and told him to no longer expect it. She was reading from a letter that C.E. LLC's primary law firm sent to her. The supposedly confidential letter from the agency director to the law firm said he would not appoint an investigator to look into the multi-million-dollar contract charges raised by C.E. and was closing the case.

"Hold on," I said loudly. "It's been my experience after working in the federal government for as many years as I did that no general or manager writes such a letter to a law firm and labels it confidential. It's not done. Something as sensitive as what C.E. brought up would be addressed by the Agency's General Counsel."

"I am sorry," she said. "I'm reading what they sent me."

C.E. chimed in, "Bonita is right. A confidential letter seems unwarranted, and General Officers never respond directly to any law firm. That's the responsibility of their general counsel. I've not heard from the agency director in response to either of my two letters to him, especially once I declared myself an official whistleblower. Why would the agency director write to the law firm and not me when I am the one that brought up the charges? This seems like more of C.E. LLC's smoke and mirror bullshit they've pulled off since the day they bid on the assets of C.E. Inc."

"Let's see a copy of that letter," I interrupted.

But the new legal advisor skirted the question and insisted that C.E. didn't have leverage any more. She suggested he stop fighting C.E. LLC. She advised that as a *pro se* (someone arguing before the court on their own behalf), C.E. could get clobbered in a hearing.

"If I can get the law firm to drop the charges, are you willing to stop fighting its client?" she asked.

"Of course, what choice do I have?" C.E. replied. "But you must remember, I'm not as much fighting C.E. LLC as I'm defending myself against their trumped-up charges in a civil complaint. They are the ones that started this!"

A few weeks after our conversation with the legal advisor, C.E. found a bulky package in our mailbox from the two law firms previously representing C.E. LLC. They had filed an amendment to their original complaint, stating that C.E. LLC had suffered actual damages because of C.E. alerting the federal agency in charge of the multi-million-dollar contract. I wanted to jump up and down and scream "the lying sons of bitches finally got their comeuppance!" But I was too unnerved to do so based on the sheer size of the document. *Here we go again; those motherfuckers don't know when to quit*, I thought.

"You best be prepared to defend yourself against this heavy-charged document," I told C.E. as we drove away from our mailbox.

"But how, Bonita, am I going to do that?" he asked quizzically.

"Leave it to me to figure that out," I answered assuredly.

After thoroughly reading the amended complaint, C.E grew even more silent than when he was ousted from C.E. LLC's board of directors. There were even more personal and withering remarks about C.E. this time around, contrasted with statements about the excellent business acumen of C.E. LLC. All the back and forth with C.E. LLC over the years was taking a toll on C.E.'s health, and the amended complaint's demand to hold a trial by jury didn't help.

As I've admitted, I am not wired like C.E. He's a polite gentleman who treats everyone with courtesy and respect and expects the same. And, because he is a man of his word, he thinks the rest of the world operates the same way. As for me, my maternal grandfather taught me the proper—genteel— way of behaving which served me well when I moved from home. After moving to New York City and later Washington, D.C. during my late twenties, I started almost immediately attending embassy parties and White House events, and after I married C.E. we often dined among some of our wealthy and influential friends and entertained even more as the wife of a General Officer, thus I had honed protocol and etiquette skills. While I lived that sophisticated and refined life, I was still the girl who would buck up and not allow herself to be pushed around by anyone. All my life, I've done that. I stood up against the racist element in my hometown, and others who came after them. So, standing up for my husband and for myself against these so-called businesspeople and their highly paid ruthless lawyers was something I was more than willing to do.

I grew up trusting no one, not even my mother because she advised me almost daily not to do so. As a youngster, I saw people kill each other just because one man gazed at another's girlfriend a bit too long. "*Que chingados miras?*" was a typical question asked around the neighborhood I grew up in. You were to look away the moment someone asked you: "What the fuck are you staring at?" If you didn't, you'd best be ready for a punch in the face, or a knife thrust at your belly. Or even a bullet to your head. That sort of cause-and-effect happened a lot in my young world.

I don't like stepping away from a fight if I'm wrongly accused. That also goes for anyone accusing my husband. Everything the two flaw firms charged him with was based on a critical document that he didn't sign. I can't say whether the law firms knew for a fact that C.E. didn't sign that document, plus another state asset sale document that was also introduced in court. All C.E. and I knew was that the forged documents were presented in court and the judge in the case accepted them. How that could have happened in a U.S. court of law makes me sick to my stomach and gives me pause about our judicial system.

C.E. did his job as a responsible citizen who witnessed wrongdoing on a multi-million-dollar government contract and blew the whistle. He didn't display a pattern of calling other federal agencies to complain about C.E. LLC or dispute any other of their contracts' legitimacy. His focus—as a whistleblower—was on the multi-million-dollar contract. The law firms had little to go on, but they did find a ton of garbage to pile into a lawsuit. And when a defendant reads all the charges and monetary claims a law firm can file, I can understand why any average person would be worried out of their wits and call it a day.

Not me. I couldn't wait to get in the legal ring with C.E. LLC's law firms. I wanted to hit back against them. "Why don't you file a counterclaim against those bastards," I urged C.E. Many unanswered questions could be challenged if you go to trial.

C.E. listened and said cautiously: "I ought to call the legal advisor and get her opinion."

She responded immediately, cautioning that C.E. would have his work cut out for him if he filed a counterclaim against C.E. LLC, but she didn't discourage him.

"We have all the time in the world," I assured her.

She said that as *pro se,* only C.E. could represent himself in the court hearing, but he could rely on others to help him prepare for it.

C.E's counterclaim was sent to the court without a problem. Still, in assisting him, I made a couple of procedural mistakes. The first thing they teach you in law school is court procedure. So, while documentation may have been loaded up with ammunition to counter C.E. LLC's charges against C.E., the procedures were killers. Many important cases have been lost because the lawyer didn't follow the court's strict guidelines. Yet C.E. wasn't about to give up. I helped clean up the mistakes and pressed on. We went back and forth with the two law firms submitting one document after another to prepare for a trial by jury, which they included in their complaint. From a legal representation perspective, everything seemed to be on the side of C.E. LLC. It was me—a non-lawyer neophyte—against three law firms with a staff of several people throwing tons of work at C.E. that I painstakingly helped him review and respond in a legal brief.

The charges against C.E. were not challenging to overturn. The problem was the Final Contract Sale Agreement that could not be relitigated because C.E. LLC had previously introduced it as evidence against C.E. The court had accepted it, but that was because the judge in the case wasn't told by C.E's lawyer that C.E. had not signed such a document. At one point, I became engaged into a shouting match over the telephone with the lead lawyer representing C.E. LLC over the Final Contract Sale Agreement. "You cannot relitigate the Contract Sale Agreement," he insisted.

"C.E. is bringing it up to defend himself against your ridiculous charges," I shot back. "If you don't want him to refer to the Contract Sale Agreement in his case documents, tell your client to stop bringing it up. Besides, there is a lot more to the document than meets the eye. Rest assured that C.E. will present his statement on the legitimacy of the document during the trial."

C.E. was headed toward a trial by jury. We met the required deadlines to hand in all the documents to the circuit court. While C.E. provided information to defend himself, C.E. LLC also had to provide information. In one vital revelation, C.E. and I discovered during the exchange of documents that C.E. LLC could not prove they paid for C.E. Inc.'s assets. The more we asked for proof, the more they stonewalled.

Even the bank did not provide positive proof to C.E. that the asset sale was consummated. The documents from the bank provided information about wire transfers made to C.E. Inc.'s loan with the bank, but it didn't show who wired those funds.

C.E. raised the question of the legitimacy of the Final Contract Sale Agreement in court documents but the two law firms representing C.E. LLC dismissed it as C.E. trying to question the legality of a document previously accepted by another civil court. I argued with C.E. LLC's lead lawyer that this was newly-discovered information that could be justly brought up in court and advised him C.E. intended to do just that.

The bespectacled, nervous lead lawyer had another problem: his name was on the official state sale document as the agent for

C.E. LLC during the sale of C.E. Inc.'s assets. When I mentioned his name appeared on a fraudulent document, he claimed he wasn't at C.E. Inc.'s offices on the day of the closing sale.

I countered: "I don't care whether or not you were there. Your name appears on the official state sale document. And that document is fraudulent because C.E. did not sign it."

The lead lawyer had nothing to add. He skipped to another subject.

In one of our last moves to bring attention to their lack of cooperation, C.E. again asked C.E. LLC to prove that they paid for C.E. Inc.'s assets and requested to subpoena the bank to provide proof of sale. All C.E. LLC came up with was a lien arrangement document between them and the bank that said the bank would release the lien on C.E. Inc.'s assets when C.E. LLC paid them $3 million by a certain time and certain date. But that document was not proof that C.E. LLC paid that amount out of their pocket. To show proof, C.E. LLC would have had to send C.E. a copy of the final lien release document from the bank, which should have been notarized, signed, and acknowledged that payment was made. But, to date, no such record of payment had been provided by C.E. LLC.

The document provided by the bank raised more questions than it answered. It showed that someone paid into part of C.E. Inc.'s loan with the bank. But the documents don't show who paid into the loan. C.E. LLC stated in the Final Contract Sale Agreement—what they call the standing legal document of the asset sale—they weren't assuming C.E. Inc.'s debts. So why did they assume the loan? And when the bank changed the rules of the asset sale by allowing C.E. LLC to pay into C.E. Inc.'s bank loan, they likely cheated its common shareholders, C.E. Levine, Pancho O'Grady and Judith Wurm, on many levels. It was the bank's responsibility to ensure that the common shareholders received the same treatment as the preferred share stockholders.

After almost a year of tis back and forth, the lead lawyer called C.E. and said his client wanted to close the case. There was too much money being spent. "Well, I suggest you have a come-to-Jesus meeting with your client since he's the one that started all this, hiring law firms from every direction to defend his cowardly self," I chimed in.

By this time, C.E. had discovered documentation that described how C.E. LLC became the owner of C.E. Inc's proprietary number as well as learning the existence of the Final Contract Sale Agreement with his signature that he didn't sign. But it was too late for C.E. to pursue exposing this information to the contracting agency of the $30 million contract since he was under a temporary court order filed by C.E. LLC lawyers aimed to prevent him from speaking to the government about the contract. And after spending thousands of dollars on a law firm that didn't help his original case against C.E. LLC, he was out of money and out of luck to further expose this fraud.

Yet in the end, I—a wanna-be lawyer with only one law school course to her name—got C.E. LLC to dismiss all the charges against C.E. This, after they came blasting heavy ammo at C.E. with three law firms, two of which employed several lawyers and staff that worked practically around the clock for almost a year. C.E. agreed to meet their demands, which amounted to no more than five items aimed to silence him. C.E, as *pro se,* spent very little money. Do the math and figure out how much money C.E. LLC paid to the law firms. C.E. was relieved to put that behind him. He was tired and becoming more and more ill by the day. I could not help but wonder, *Will this dark angel of misfortune ever leave us?*

Chapter **7**

God Shows Up

> I asked God, "Why are you taking me through
> troubled water?"
> He replied, "Because your enemies can't
> swim. - Author Unknown

In the culture I grew up in, when something terrible happened, it was caused by one of four things. Either you had angered the Virgin Mary, or crossed Jesus, or God was punishing you, or someone had cursed you. At one point in our financial crisis, I felt all four applied to me.

"Hail Mary, Full of Grace, the Lord is with thee" were pretty much the first English words I learned. After that, everything I did daily was meant to satisfy "La Virgensita," the Blessed Mother. Everyone around me warned to never disappoint the Blessed Mother or her son Jesus Christ, for I'd end up in Purgatory if I did. That belief was instilled in me almost daily by every relative, every neighbor, and every friend, but more so by Father Pete, the priest of the Sacred Heart Catholic Church on the town's southside.

I recall my Nanita Lucia's frightening tone when she repeated the story of La Virgensita's apparition before a young indigenous man, Juan Diego, in central Mexico many, many centuries earlier—December 9, 1531, to be exact. It seemed to be a scary and mysterious event, and I wished for the Blessed Mother's presence so that I'd be blessed for always, just like Juan Diego, who ended up a saint after he witnessed La Virgensita's apparition.

But when C.E. and I lost everything we worked for, I didn't have any hope the Blessed Mother would make an appearance to assure me that my life would be okay. Could it be those certain decisions I made as a young woman were coming home to roost with the force of the spiritual power? Some of my past sins were shameful to the point where I cannot and will not repeat them. If I was still a practicing Catholic, they would likely be of the Purgatory level, maybe even Hell. Those decisions were front and center with all I believed spiritually: La Virgensita, Jesus, God Almighty, the Maker of Heaven and Earth, and the Holy Spirit. Why else was I suffering so much emotional pain? There wasn't a day that I wasn't on my knees, begging my spiritual guides for forgiveness. Yet I had a depressing feeling that forgiveness would not come easy.

Nanita Lucia often warned that no one leaves this earth without paying for their sins. From her rickety rocking chair, she'd tell story after story of people she knew who had committed acts against God's teachings, only to pay dearly. "*Quieren que Dios no sabe lo que eserio, pero Dios todo sabe y todo se paga.*" she'd laugh. "They think God doesn't know what they did. But God knows everything and pay they will."

If my penance for bad behavior was everlasting, I became convinced that my life would become perpetual bad luck and suffering. Yet, at the same time I felt that with such bad luck in our lives, bad behavior notwithstanding, surely someone had put a curse on me, or C.E. or both. I thought of visiting a fortune teller as we called them back in the day to ward off the curse, just like my mother did years earlier. But times had changed. Fortune tellers charged a lot more than when my mother paid them a visit for the basic tarot card reading along with advice on how to ward off the curse which could consist of some far-out ideas. Regardless of how ridiculous the ideas, I wasn't in any position to afford to visit a fortune teller.

So, I took my curse research to the internet. I became frantic, reading up on ways to find ways to kill off the evil spirit. The cures ran the gamut from hanging horseshoes at the entrance of your home to burning bay leaves inside the house at a certain time of the day. So many cockamamie ideas, I didn't know if I was coming or going. I became almost maniacal, never mind the risk of burning down my house. Warding off the evil spirits to change our luck became an all-consuming exercise but, thank God, a short-lived obsession.

Bad luck seemed to be all around us right after C.E. lost his corporate job. Our credit rating sank, we lost of our beloved city townhome and most of our possessions. We lost our financial way. You name the bad luck, we had it all around us. And, if things weren't bad enough, I began hearing strange noises in our city home. Then it partnered with an odor of sulfur to stink to high heaven. I was convinced our city house had been overtaken by an evil spirit, the same place we believed years earlier was a blessing from above because it was the first home we came to own.

About one year after losing his CEO job, C.E, television remote in hand, was channel surfing one day. He pressed pause on the remote to pour himself a cup of coffee. The channel he had paused on displayed a slim young man with a head full of shiny dark hair better coiffed than mine. The preacher seemed a diminutive figure at the podium in his enormous church. His words to the packed church seemed strictly directed toward C.E and me. He assured his audience that their lives would get better no matter how bad things seemed. He preached that God loved all his children. And that, if we found ourselves in a dark place, God would not leave us there forever. His words were inspiring, but when you are about to lose everything—maybe not down to our underwear, but most everything else—like we were about to, neither of us accepted the preacher's assurances. There seemed to be too much darkness in our lives to think God would ever shine a light on us!

My pessimism about the preacher's words didn't abate. But tuning in to his popular TV show, Sunday after Sunday, I came to accept and understand that what happened to us was God's will. The more I listened to the preacher, the better I felt, and the better I felt, the more I came to accept our circumstances, hate notwithstanding. Hate is not in God's vocabulary, but I couldn't help myself. Hatred and revenge had consumed my soul. Then one day, I popped open a bottle of Honest Tea. The lid, like all the tea's caps, had an inscription. This one, a quote from the Chinese philosopher Confucius made me pause and think: "Before you embark on a journey of revenge, dig two graves." At that moment, I believed God was sending me a message to stop seeking revenge. But, I figured, the truth was something else, and that became my quest.

If the blessed mother is disappointed in you and Jesus isn't happy with you, God Almighty is still unhappier. And when the Holy Spirit is nowhere to be found, who's left to turn to? With bills piling up and no financial relief in sight, it felt like C.E. and I swam against a riptide sweeping us out to sea into deep waters, without a boat and without life preservers. It was scary as hell! And, without much of a religious foundation, I didn't feel equipped to figure out how to reach God to save us.

Although I was baptized a Catholic, my early church-going days were few at best. And, when I did walk into the Sacred Heart Catholic Church, Father Pete's sermon made zero sense to me. Catechism classes were supposed to teach us the way of the Lord, but all that registered was the punishment I suffered from the nuns. My knuckles were black and blue from the strikes they took from the wooden ruler or whatever stick they had at the moment. I learned very little other than to be terrified of the nuns. Our parish priest wasn't any different. Instead of showing us the blessings of God, he seemed full of an all-consuming anger. Constantly shouting at the altar boys, ordering the nuns around and about, and admonishing his congregation for some untoward behavior or religious lapse (as judged by him as God's representative). Some of us joked that Father Pete was angry all the time because "he wasn't getting any." We may have been right.

There weren't any rumors of sexual abuse or otherwise inappropriate behavior about Father Pete, which wasn't the case with priests who followed him. One of them molested a beloved family member who was barely six years old. Even though my sister and brother-in-law suspected something, they kept quiet about their son. How could they accuse a man who they believed was on a first-name basis with Jesus of molesting their child? The Catholic Church would have its members believe priests held the keys to their entrance into Heaven. So, my sister and brother-in-law did not speak out. Instead, they allowed a predator to molest my nephew until his teen years, then the priest was transferred to another parish where he was reported to have molested even more young boys. Years later, I, along with the rest of America, learned my nephew wasn't the only one robbed of childhood innocence and happiness by priests who preyed on the young to satisfy their sick sexual desires. One of the most difficult things in my life was to look my sister and her husband in the eye, knowing they allowed the priest to sexually abuse their son. And it was even more difficult to accept the old sexual predator as a man of the cloth, one of God's chosen.

It was especially emotionally painful to watch my nephew go into a dark period so early in his life. He would spend hours in his room with the windows closed and the lights turned off. He rarely stepped out, and he would keep his head down the whole time when he did. The priest damaged that young child's self-image and wrecked him emotionally. Yet, with all that darkness in his life, my nephew accepted Jesus Christ as his savior. He was determined to make a better life for himself. He was happy in a relationship with a very giving and supportive man, and he was recognized as one of the best elementary teachers in the country. Yet the darkness never quite left him. When he contracted HIV/AIDS, he was in a state of shock and fright, blaming himself for his life choices. We spent hours on the phone while I reassured him that God loved him. I learned much from him while I was going through my dark period, except there was no one to reassure me that God loved me— well, except the TV preacher.

Developing faith and sustaining it can be difficult when you have little or no religious foundation. In my family, except for a baptism or marriage ceremony or funeral, we rarely stepped into Father Pete's church. "*Para que vamos a la iglesia, si todos nos vamos a ir con el demonio,*" my Nanita Lucia said often. Her words meant that there was no point in going to church since we were all going to Hell anyway. Every time I heard her repeat those words, I felt like saying, "*Speak for yourself, you old goat,*" but thought better of it, lest I ended up in Heaven a lot earlier than I planned (or Hell according to my wise old grandmother.) I must have been in high school when I first saw a book called The Holy Bible. I give credit to Father Pete for our home not having a Bible and my mother for following his unsolicited advice. He told us time and time again that we needn't own a Bible since he would be the one to tell us what it said, anointing himself as the expert to interpret the spiritual book as if his congregation wasn't capable of doing that for themselves.

My mother was the single-parent head of our household and the only breadwinner. She also rarely stepped inside the church. Maybe she might have, had she not labored in the town's busiest café for nearly forty years, unable to take time off. The café owners for whom she cooked and baked delicious food every day were, in a word, merciless. She was expected to show up for work every day or not have a job. Paid vacation and sick leave were unknown benefits in my mother's working world. Hell, even I fell victim to the café owners lack of regard for their workers. One morning, while I lay sound asleep on my mother's bed, which I shared with her when her boyfriend was absent, the male owner of the café walked into the house without knocking. His booming voice woke me up and I was startled to see the tall blue-eyed man standing by the side of the bed, barking orders, "Get up pronto, your mother said for you to come with me to wash dishes and clean the café," while yanking the bed covers off me. He didn't allow me time to wash my face and brush my teeth, hurriedly pushing me out of the house while I managed to grab some old dress to put over my pajamas. *"This bolillo pendejo has some nerve,"* I said to myself. But that was all I could do was talk to myself. I ended up washing dishes the entire summer from 4:00 a.m. to 2:00 p.m. every day, including weekends. Sometimes I worked longer if the afternoon shift dishwasher didn't show up, which was often. It was a good thing he found a permanent dishwasher because, if he hadn't, he was expecting me to drop out of school and work full time. I was disappointed that my mother didn't discourage him.

My Nanita Lucia was the church-going exception. She went every chance she got but more to partake of the free church food than pray. Not that she was impoverished. She just loved other people's cooking, grabbing, and nibbling every food item in reach and then grading it as if she were a food contest judge. Fortunately, or unfortunately, she passed on that food habit to me. I love doing the same thing no matter the event— embassy party, birthday party, White House event. All the food is up for grabs the moment I enter the room. In the aftermath of C.E. losing his job, I did it more out of necessity than for fun. I found myself in a situation where I routinely stuffed as much food as I could into several cocktail napkins that I stored in my large Chanel bag. Food that would last several days for both of us to eat.

My grandfather, Don Daniel, may have been baptized a Christian, but his roots were Jewish. He came from a long line of Spanish Jews that fled Spain to Mexico to avoid religious persecution. While he may have been baptized a Catholic, he never took one step into our town's church as long as I knew him. And he paid for that decision. When he passed away, Father Pete refused to administer the last rites to my grandfather or admit his remains into his church. Father Pete didn't recognize my grandfather as a member of his congregation, and some in town whispered that the reason was his Jewish roots.

So, at a very young age, I questioned my Catholic faith, and I never felt that telling my sins and utmost secrets to some stranger would save me. Who was he, anyway, that I should tell my utmost secrets? In Father Pete's case, he made it a habit of revealing the sins of some in his congregation during Sunday Mass. He didn't reveal the names. But he didn't have to, we all knew who he was talking about. Like many others, I felt I'd be disrespecting God if I even thought about questioning the priest's intentions, let alone denouncing my Catholic faith. Yet, once I learned of my nephew's molestation, I asked myself, "*Why I should confess my sins to a man who had committed sins far greater than mine?*" And when my *Buelito* Daniel was denied his last rites by Father Pete, that did it. I left my Catholic faith. Years later, I became an Episcopalian along with C.E. We heard all kinds of remarks and jabs about our new faith. Some referred to us as "Catholics that can read." Others called us "Whiskypalians." But it didn't bother us. The church's Mother Jenny welcomed us with open arms and laughingly said, "If it wasn't for Catholics marrying Baptists, we wouldn't have a church."

C.E. had a rigorous religious and a more stable upbringing far different from mine. Although his father was Jewish, his mother was a Christian and she was determined to raise C.E.

and his two sisters, Barbara and Sarah, in a Bible-led church. Almost from birth, C.E.'s mother read her three children the Bible daily. All three attended Bible school every Sunday and they, along with their parents, Stanley and Martha Levine, attended church revivals all over the state. Over his early life, C.E. probably attended more church revivals than Elvis Presley gave concerts. He knew all the words to many church hymns intended to make you feel closer to God. And, because of his strict Christian upbringing, I felt C.E. was saved and was convinced he would save me, too, when our financial lives collapsed.

If the Catholic Church taught me anything, it was that Jesus told his followers not to fight back, but instead to turn the other cheek. But in the *barrio* where I grew up, knife fights were routine, and you did not back down or run away. An incidental glance, or an accidental shove, would bring out the weapons: little knives, short knives, long knives, even guns. All intended to cut you up or blow you away and teach you a lesson. Never disrespect a fellow Mexican from the *barrio*. I can't remember the number of knife fights I witnessed, and that was before I entered First Grade. I began carrying a small pocketknife when I was around eight or nine years old. I learned to fight back or die! And that brings me back to what was happening to me as a grown-up: I was in the fight of my life when C.E. lost his job and his company. But bringing a knife to a gunfight would not get me anywhere against a powerful bank and law firms that would stop at nothing to protect their client.

It's a human tendency to blame everyone around you for your misfortune. I blamed those that sold and those that bought C.E.'s company's assets. I blamed C.E. I blamed myself. And I blamed God. "Why did you do this, God?" became an unrelenting question that consumed my life day in and day out. As our financial lives collapsed, everything in my world was failing, too. My self-respect waned, my courage diminished, and my confidence leaked from me like a balloon with a pinhole. Self-pity and fear replaced all that I lost.

It took a while to realize it was up to me to stand up, not only for myself, but also for C.E., who was on the verge of a near breakdown. I had to figure a way for both of us to have a reason to get up in the morning and face the world. I set out to learn the truth of the asset sale and concentrated on those who accused and convinced my husband he was such a loser of a manager that the bank was forced to sell C.E. Inc's assets for a mere $3.4 million, yet knowing that the company was valued in the millions and had even more millions in pre-awarded contracts under C. E.'s leadership.

The more our financial life collapsed, the more frightened C.E. and I became about our future. What would happen to us? Would we lose everything and become homeless? So many questions, but so few answers.

In the vernacular, I understood the TV star preacher telling us Sunday after Sunday that God did this to C.E. and me for a reason. I was up to us to figure out why and do something about it. However, it's not that simple. It's hard to look in the mirror when you're guilt-ridden over past sins and frightened to face the future. Amidst all this, a friend invited me to a book signing and lecture by a famous writer. It was a relief to turn away from the constant emotional pain I felt day after day to listen to the famous woman talk about her latest book. A long-time admirer of her writings, I felt I knew even more of her after spending a delightful evening dining with her parents and a well-known senator and his wife many years earlier.

In her talk, the author mentioned her relationship with God. My ears opened since I was in the process of establishing my own relationship with the Almighty. But I interpreted the author as essentially holding God responsible for life's woes, questioning why He would allow pain and suffering to happen. I wanted to jump out of my seat and shout: "God doesn't hurt people. People hurt people!" After what C.E. had experienced, I felt I was an authority on the subject. I thought of past events that helped convince me of such. Who brought down the Persian Empire? It was the work of an army led by one person, Alexander the Great. And I thought about all the religious sacrifices against men, women, and children made by the Aztecs, led by one person, Moctezuma I. What about the Holocaust, where six million Jews and others were murdered by the Nazis and led by one, Adolph Hitler? Humans are responsible for all good and evil on this earth. It's up to God to sort us out, whether here on earth, in the afterlife, or both.

The people who ended up with my husband's company's assets and its proprietary number could have kept their word and hired C.E. for the initially proposed time and price and follow federal acquisition contract regulations. They made choices. God did not do that. God didn't bully and shame C.E. one day and praise him the next.

I don't believe God told the bank representatives, Kane Hunter and Barry Liar, to ignore a higher bid from two other companies and take much less money for the company's assets.

I don't believe God told the owners of C.E. LLC to copy C.E.'s signature page from the Contract Sale Agreement framework and insert into the Final Contract Sale Agreement document.

I don't believe God told C.E. LLC to present—as the Final Contract Sale Agreement—a document that C.E. never reviewed, approved, or signed.

I don't believe God told Simon Green, Horace Steele, and Charlie Kaka to dismiss C.E. from their company's board immediately after he signed the Contract Sale Agreement framework document.

I don't believe God told C.E. LLC to take the federally-assigned proprietary number from C.E. Inc., an entity they didn't buy and own, which in turn yielded them millions in federal contracts they didn't rightfully own based on federal acquisition regulations.

I don't believe God told someone to forge C.E.'s signature on the state's official sale asset document.

The bank's fiduciary responsibility was to ensure that the common share stockholders, C.E. Levine, and his two company officers, Pancho O'Grady and Judith Wurm, were compensated based on the company's worth and earned contracts and to sell the company according to that value. Yet they came up with a questionable legal binding contract sale agreement framework document and threatened C.E. that the bank would sue him for violating his fiduciary responsibility if he didn't sign the document.

The buyers of C.E. Inc.'s assets, Simon Green, Horace Steele, and Charlie Kaka, initially assured C.E. and his two officers they planned to keep the management team in place. Yet, a few days before the final asset sale, Horace Steele announced that Gustavo Feo, would become the president of C.E. LLC. It was unknown to C.E. at the time that Feo was a close friend of Steele's and one who had zero experience in running a company of C.E. Inc.'s magnitude and potential.

The attorney hired by the bank to carry out the asset sale, Sean Sneek, criticized C.E. for his company's financial status, yet simultaneously told him how valuable he would be to the new company owners of C.E. LLC and urged him to take the board seat offered to him. He kept asking C.E.: "What's not to like?" several times to convince C.E. to sign the contract sale agreement framework document.

And there was Archer Knave, who conducted the bank's commissioned sale study report to show the negative worth of the company, to justify selling C.E. Inc.'s assets at $3.4 million, only to learn from the report's findings that the company was worth at least $30 to $35 million and had a pipeline of close to $150 million in revenue over five years!

There was plenty that lay before C.E. that might have changed the course of our lives and that of many other people. But he was outgunned and outnumbered. Through this entire process, C.E. didn't have a lawyer to protect his six, as the old military saying goes, while the new buyers of his company's assets were protected not only by a group of lawyers, but also by the bank, the preferred stockholder of C.E. Inc.

So, there you have it. It wasn't God but red-blooded humans who ended C.E. Inc., which was a well-run company doing good things for its employees, its clients, and for America's economy. I believe and accept that what happened to us was God's way of telling us He loved us. The emotional pain both C.E. and I suffered was God's way of teaching us lessons from our past indiscretions, while protecting us from a future that wasn't as bleak as we thought. So, over the years, I've listened more carefully to the television preacher's words. And I've come to feel as protected by God as he protected Shadrach, Meshach, and Abednego. The three young Hebrew men described in Chapter Three of the Book of Daniel were thrown into a fiery furnace by Nebuchadnezzar, king of Babylon. But God saved them, as he did C.E. and me.

One bright summer day, after having tuned in to the preacher's show for the umpteenth time, I stood in the kitchen talking out loud to no one that, no matter how much suffering we were experiencing, I believed in God and always would. At that point, the wine cork that sat on the kitchen counter from a bottle we had just popped open started moving, rolling back and forth. There weren't any windows open, no draft coming into the house. The air was as still as I'd ever experienced.

I looked at C.E., wide-eyed, and said, "Did you see that?"

Just as he was about to answer, the cork moved again, swaying back and forth, back and forth several more times. We both felt a sense of the Holy Spirit's presence. We embraced and wept, convinced that God had paid us a visit. I believe God speaks to all of us. His voice guides us to make the best decisions about our lives. It's called revelation! All that is required on our part is to pay close attention to our faith in God Almighty. *Faith is believing what God has said and then acting upon it.*

One day, after a heavy rainfall, I witnessed the longest and most colorful double rainbow I'd ever seen. It seemed to extend across the county. The bright colors seemed to seep right into the ground. Even though a pot of gold didn't materialize, an old friend appeared after more than twenty years and offered me a much-needed job. My friend was an angel from above who appeared out of nowhere and in the nick of time to save us from total financial disaster.

A few months after my friend hired me, another friend introduced us to a woman who'd written a book based on Psalm 91. An entire book on one Psalm? I questioned. C.E. and I met with the author at a hotel near one of the busiest airports in the country. Upon learning of our plight, she prayed with us. It seemed odd praying in the lobby of a hotel. I probably would have giggled at the sight in earlier days, but I felt God's presence again that night. The author seemed to be another angel sent from above. The words on the back cover grabbed my attention: "He shall cover you with His feathers, and under his wings, you shall find protection; His faithfulness shall be your shield and wall."

I wasn't so sure we'd ever regain our once-prosperous life. Still, after reading those prophetic words, I became familiar with the entire Psalm 91. Something in me changed. I pivoted to a more positive stage, believing that C.E. and I were regaining our spirit and raising our souls to the Almighty.

It's easy to think the worst when traveling through life's deepest and darkest corridors. You feel worthless, a loser, while terror takes over. Before you know it, you begin to think your life is not worth a dime and you begin to think of ways to end it. But God's visit to our country home brought me out of the darkness. And Psalm 91 was God's message that I was welcome in His fortress and that He would protect me. So, my life I once thought of ending became relevant once again. Every day, I feel God's presence. His grace lifting off the dark veil that covered my life for many years. God helped restore my life; I did the rest. I began to take back my life, not like before, but better! I stayed in the game and kept my eye on the ball and kicked the hell out of that angel of darkness, right out of my life and that of C.E.'s. And, like my Jewish ancestors, I placed a mezuzah on the side of our front door. I touch it every time I enter to let God in and protect our home from any bad angel trying to get in.

Chapter **8**

The Conspiracy

> "The individual is handicapped by coming face-to-face with a conspiracy so monstrous he cannot believe it exists." - J. Edgar Hoover

In our capitalistic government, vulture-like people thrive and make millions capitalizing on calamities and misfortune. For these types, the idea of human suffering holds no place in their version of the great human endeavor, be it Christian or otherwise. Instead, their sole gratification is to feed and profit off the suffering caused by the government shifting its priorities and stopping funding in one area while funding another. And our banking laws have developed over the centuries to allow banks the widest latitude to make money, ensuring that when they seem to lose money, they in fact make a profit.

And so we are back to the artfully-orchestrated plan by several characters that would serve to destroy C.E.'s reputation and our financial well-being. The bank's representative, Kane Hunter, looms large at the heart of this plan. The prime insider of C.E. Inc. is identified only after asking about certain events. It seems that the bank became the facilitator of this plan. More on that as we go along.

The events necessary for the plan to become a reality were:

C.E. Inc. missed a covenant of their loan agreement with the lender, the bank. Missing the covenant was severe for a business being rebuilt. Still, it was easily rectified with a tax rebate that arrived that year. However, much to management's dismay—and to the business's detriment—the bank swept all the tax rebate into their own pocket to pay down C.E. Inc.'s bank loan, or at least that's what they said at the time.

The combination owner/lender bank had developed the habit of managing C.E. Inc.'s operating cash. In short, they continually refused to provide the capital required to purchase the raw materials necessary to produce critical items already contracted by the federal government, thus, straining not only the company but its suppliers as well. This progressed to where

C.E. Inc. had to explain to the buyer, the federal government, that it would be a few days late with one or more of their orders.

Even in the face of all the above, C.E. Inc. continued to have excellent relations with its government buyers. The products were of the highest quality, and the buyer placed much trust in C.E. Levine to always deliver the products on time. As the rumors of a government shutdown increased, buyers within the government continually told C.E. that his company's products were sorely needed by the military and to pass that information on to its lender, the bank. Federal contract specialists assured C.E.: "Do not be nervous. We have funding set aside for your products, and that money is ready to be released as soon as the government shutdown is lifted."

So, as its management assessed the situation, C.E. Inc., though it had debt, remained a good investment for the bank. The company had already rebuilt its production business and was well on the way to more significant business with the U.S. government. Yet the bank was keen on selling off C.E. Inc. and asked C.E. to find a buyer for the company at around $30 million.

Interestingly, within days of the bank's decision to sell C.E. Inc., the CEO and COO of the Midwest company that C.E. Inc. had cooperated with on a few small product lines visited the company's headquarters, completely unannounced. C.E and Pancho O'Grady discussed working together on future projects and gave them a tour of the production facility, but both seemed inattentive and hurried.

Now, bear in mind that the Midwest company had been told the price would be around $30 million, if anyone was interested. Neither C.E. nor Pancho O'Grady had shared this information with anyone else except Judith Wurm because of what was considered the extreme sensitivity surrounding the bank's decision to sell. One cannot ignore the timing of the bank's decision to advise C.E. they were willing to sell for around $30 million and that the Midwest company's executives appeared unannounced at C.E. Inc.'s headquarters within only a few days. Coincidental? Maybe yes, maybe no. Yet, instead of taking C.E.'s offer of $30 million for the entire company, the Midwestern company only a few months later decided to pay $50 million instead to C.E. LLC for the same company's contracts and products that were included in C.E.'s offer.

Along with the bank's decision to sell C.E. Inc. as a whole and, later, only its assets, came the tightening of the purse strings by the bank on the company. Importantly, though, C.E. Inc. continued to make payments on their loan, even with high interest rates, due to considerable assistance from the government contracting officers who found money to fund ongoing projects.

Still, the bank had hired Archer Knave's firm to manage the sale of the company. The same Archer Knave who announced to C.E. and his two officers that a firm in Delaware had a high interest in C.E. Inc. and he could get them to visit the company within a day. The bank also hired the law firm—represented by Sean Sneek who had assisted the bank in previous Chapter Eleven proceedings to help in the sale. Sneek told Knave that the sale 'process' was extremely important to the bank. It would proceed much slower than what was visualized by Knave's company. Turns out the process was merely slowed but not stopped.

Before Knave appeared on the scene, C.E. Inc. had received a bid from a northeastern firm to purchase the entire company. But the bid was ignored by the bank. A few months after the company's legitimate interest was discarded by the bank, Knave's company was hired and he brought in two companies—

purported buyers—to visit C. E. Inc. headquarters and meet with its management team. Except neither were industrial-type companies nor had they ever done business with the government, let alone managed multimillion-dollar contracts. They were small companies, each offering less than one million dollars. And there was the offer from a major industrial company that was passed over by the bank through Knave. Theirs was a higher offer than the one from C.E. LLC.

During discussions with C.E. LLC, which had even less industrial experience than the two other key bidders, the bank reset the selling price far from the $30 million that C.E., as CEO of C.E. Inc., had been advised was its value and asking price. When the price changed dramatically to $3.4 million for assets only, C.E. Levine and Pancho O'Grady told Sean Sneek they could likely get funding to buy the assets and continue the company as an operating entity. Sneek rejected their proposal outright. It seemed the bank had revoked the Right of First Refusal clause in the contract between itself and C.E. Inc.'s officers. And the third officer, Judith Wurm, backed up the bank instead of siding with her colleagues. This prevented C.E. and Pancho O'Grady from borrowing funds or raising capital to acquire their company in a management buyout. Besides this, the internal support for the company executives to buy their company quickly waned when the two other management team members balked. Unknown to C.E., both O'Grady and Wurm had been offered employment contracts with C.E. LLC.

C.E. LLC may have convinced the federal government that their company and C.E. Inc. were the same company, which allowed them to acquire C.E. Inc.'s federally-assigned proprietary number. That subterfuge enabled C.E. LLC to end up with C.E. Inc.'s million dollars of contracts that didn't belong to them and which they turned around and sold for even more millions of dollars to a third party, a publicly-traded company in the Midwest.

Someone made a copy of C.E.'s and Gustavo Feo's signature page from the contract sale agreement framework document and inserted the copy into the Final Contract Sale Agreement, which had a different date from the framework document. C.E. never reviewed, approved, and signed the Final Contract Sale Agreement document, a document that was used against him in a civil court case.

Someone forged C.E.'s signature on the official state asset sale document. The document stated that C.E. was to decide how C.E. LLC would pay $3.4 million for C.E. Inc.'s assets, but that payment wasn't made to C.E. by C.E. LLC.

To execute the legitimacy of the Final Contract Sale Agreement, C.E. LLC used a single page with C.E.'s signature that did not include a date because Charlie Kaka, C.E. LLC's company's board chairman, asked C.E. not to date it. That signature page was then included along with a separate signature page of the three board members—Green, Steele and Kaka—in the minutes of C.E. LLC's first board meeting to indicate that C.E. and the other board members met to acknowledge the Final Contract Sale Agreement. C.E. was told by Charlie Kaka that his signature signified his acceptance of the new company's board membership, but as C.E. later learned, his signature meant he was acknowledging the Final Contract Sale Agreement, a document that wasn't presented to him that day. It would be several more years before C.E. saw the actual final document.

The bank changed the asset sale agreement terms between C.E. Inc. and C.E. LLC by allowing C.E. LLC to pay into part of C.E. Inc.'s bank loan. To change the terms of the asset sale, the bank would have had to seek approval from C.E. and his two company officers, especially since all three never resigned from C.E. Inc., an entity that was in operation a year after its asset sale. Besides, this action on the part of the bank was contrary to the so-called Final Contract Sale Agreement in which C.E. LLC declared it was not absorbing C.E. Inc's debt.

Both the bank and C.E. LLC claimed that C.E. LLC paid close to $3.4 million into C.E. Inc's loan with the bank. However, there is no proof that C.E. LLC wired payments into C.E. Inc's bank loan. And why did the bank only allow C.E. LLC to pay less than half of the remaining balance on C.E. Inc's loan with the bank? It makes one wonder why the bank didn't give that type of deal to C.E. Inc., which had years of experience in the industrial field and had a proven record of winning millions in federal contracts.

Two weeks after he signed the contract sale agreement framework document, C.E. was fired from the C.E. LLC's board by its chairman, Charlie Kaka, and its other board members, Simon Green and Horace Steele.

The plan was essentially complete. C.E. Levine, who had built a backlog of very lucrative U.S. Government contracts, was out with nothing at 78 years old. Not long after the asset sale, C.E. LLC sold itself to a much larger Midwest company for $50 million. C.E. LLC did not invent a single new product or bring in new contacts. All of the contracts they sold to the Midwest company had been pre-awarded to C.E. Inc. through its federally-assigned proprietary number which had not been fully awarded at the time of the asset sale, thus they weren't rightfully C.E. LLC's to sale to a third party.

This plan likely required collusion to succeed. Those involved were likely the two executives from the Midwest company, Martin Crook and Joseph Rich, along with Simon Green and Horace Hunter, Charlie Kaka, Sean Sneek, Archer Knave, Gustavo

Feo, Judith Wurm and the biggest pigs in this mud wallow, Kane Hunter and Barry Liar, from the bank.

It's my opinion that these individuals ran a deceptive shell game scheme, but for what purpose? Perhaps for pure greed and self-enrichment. The bank, as the judge acknowledged, started all this. The bank began by planning to sell the entirety of C.E. Inc., then changed the sale to assets only. Its officials rushed the asset sale while ignoring higher bids from other companies. And in the process created a situation whereby no other companies would be considered to purchase the assets except for the newly formed company, C.E. LLC. They sold to a company formed overnight that didn't appear to have the capital to purchase the entire company. To accommodate C.E. LLC's lack of funds and zero reputation in the industrial field, the bank justified their decision to sell off C.E. Inc.'s assets by claiming that C.E. Inc. was in dire straits, blaming C.E. for its downfall and claiming their only recourse was to sell to the lowest bidder, C.E. LLC. While the asset sale did not include buying C.E. Inc.'s experienced workforce, C.E. LLC somehow ended up with the workforce and lied to the world that their company had years of experience in the industrial field.

The new company, owned by C.E. LLC, presented C.E. with a consulting agreement, only to reduce its original price in a take-it-or-leave-it ploy to squeeze out C.E. They, along with the bank, developed a contract sale agreement framework document with very little detail and coerced him into signing it through the threat of a lawsuit by the bank. Afraid to be sued, C.E. signed it. C.E. asked when he would see a Final Contract Sale Agreement to review and approve before agreeing to sign it. But neither C.E. LLC nor the bank presented him or his COO, Pancho O'Grady, with such a document to sign during the day of the asset sale.

Instead, C.E. LLC developed a Final Contract Sale Agreement document based on the original framework document, but rather than have C.E. and his two other officers review it, approve it, and sign it, someone took the signature page of the three officers and the signature page of C.E. LLC's incoming president, Gustavo Feo, along with C.E.'s signature from the contract sale agreement framework, presenting it as if all the parties had seen and signed the final document.

Someone forged C.E.'s signature on the official state asset sale document. That document said that C.E. was to receive $3.4 million for his company's assets from C.E. LLC, but that never happened. Instead, C.E. LLC claimed they paid into C.E. Inc.'s loan with the bank, totaling about $6.4 million, but the bank allowed them to pay only approximately $3.4 million.

C.E. LLC freely took C.E. Inc.'s proprietary number. The proprietary number was worth millions because C.E. Inc. had close to $50 million in federal contracts at the time of the asset sale that it had won under that number. The only way for C.E. LLC to legally acquire the proprietary number belonging to C.E.'s company would have been if they had purchased the entity, not just its assets. C.E. Inc.'s proprietary number could not be considered an asset by C.E. LLC, since it's a necessary mechanism assigned by the government to enable an entity to legally bid on federal contracts.

According to the Final Contract Sale Agreement, C.E. Inc. was supposed to be dissolved 10 days after the asset sale. But that did not happen. Instead, C.E. LLC kept C.E. Inc. alive for more than a year after the asset sale, an entity they did not purchase or own.

C.E. LLC sold itself and 'other interests' almost fifteen months after the asset sale to a much larger publicly-traded company from the Midwest for about $50 million. Along with the sale, the Midwest company acquired the federal proprietary number, which belonged to C.E. Inc. Since their acquisition of C.E. LLC, the Midwest company has earned huge profits from the millions in federal contracts they got when they bought C.E. LLC which are tied to a federally-assigned proprietary number that does not belong to them and that never belonged to C.E. LLC.

C.E. LLC took over a thriving business that they didn't build, while calling into question C.E.'s management skills and even his honorable and heroic military service.

Growing up, my family and our neighbors didn't have much, but everyone worked to maintain a decent quality of life. No one cheated anyone for anything. I may have allowed the foreman of our fruit and vegetable work crew to throw in a few extra pounds when my wooden crate was weighed, but that additional amount was paid to our foreman's granddaughter for the soft drinks and Mexican pastries she sold me on credit during the week. That was innocent. But what happened to my husband, C.E., was not innocent. Yet if it hadn't been for C.E. suing C.E. Inc. and C.E. LLC, and C.E. LLC suing him in return, the details of the asset sale might never have surfaced. And I wouldn't have had this conspiracy tale to write.

> *But what I do, I will also continue to do, that I may cut off the opportunity from those who desire an opportunity to be regarded just as we are in the things of which they boast. For such are false apostles, deceitful workers, transforming themselves into apostles of Christ. And no wonder! For Satan himself transforms himself into an angel of light.*
>
> *2 Corinthians 11:12-14, The New King James Version*

Chapter **9**

No Good Ending

> "If you wake up for a moment and look around at life, you will observe that nothing here lasts, nothing works out. There are no happy endings. All accomplishments are washed away by death or by the next moment."
> — Frederick Lindeman, First Viscount Cherwell

Pancho O'Grady walked in carrying a bottle of expensive red wine under one arm and an even higher-priced one under his other arm. He was "loaded for bear," as he liked to say, and ready to party. I hadn't seen him happier. "You look great, man!" he hollered at C.E., who was sitting in his favorite toile Chinoiserie-covered French chair in front of the television screen that was so wide it practically swallowed up our entire kitchen. Pancho's words brought a broad smile to C.E.'s face. He knew he didn't look good. He had lost a lot of weight since the last time Pancho visited us about five months earlier. In that short period, C.E.'s body lost a lot of muscle mass and he became partially immobile. He was practically unrecognizable. But Pancho chose to think and say otherwise. He made C.E. feel good and that was all that mattered. "Take your pick, Bonita, which bottle shall we crack open first?" he said. Although C.E. was no longer drinking, he nonetheless enjoyed watching Pancho and me ooh and aah over the fine wine that we sipped throughout the evening until it disappeared.

We spent a memorable evening talking and arguing about everything, from politics to military force structure. Naturally, as a matter of course, we talked about how both C.E. and Pancho were deceived by a group of self-serving, evil, and demonic people, which is how they referred to those involved in the asset sale of C.E. Inc. "Those motherfuckers," Pancho said laughingly. He was no longer bitter and kicking himself for failing to detect their conspiracy. He was in the happiest of moods about his new lease on life based on a health report that revealed he was in great shape.

Being with Pancho and C.E. reminded me that I've always enjoyed the company of male friends. That probably had to do with my childhood experiences with my older brother and his *hermanos* or brothers as he called them. There would be about ten of us at any given time who raced our bikes the two miles from our homes to town to see who could ride over the railroad tracks without being hit by the train right after it took off from the station. We'd hunt for rattlesnakes, and end their lives with our BB-guns. And play tag and hide-and-seek until the sun crept down to warm the other side of the earth. And, as I matured, my friends continued to be mostly males, even after I married C.E. One time I took C.E. to a Super Bowl party, and it shocked him that there wasn't a single female present. He came to like my friends and soon realized they were my *hermanos*— brothers, my protectors, just like the ones I grew up with in Southern California. Later in our marriage, when we would host dinner parties, it was not unusual to find me drinking brandy and smoking cigars, telling racy jokes, and talking sports with C.E. and our male guests. Meanwhile, our female guests would remain in a separate room sipping coffee and sharing food recipes or photos of their latest grandchild. I couldn't have been happier then, as I couldn't be happier on this evening sharing all kinds of stories with C.E. and Pancho on our back deck, which had a clear view of the wide-open sky that was decorated with contrails from one direction to the other. We'd point to the seemingly tiny airplanes leading the contrails while trying to outguess each other about where they'd taken off from and where they were possibly headed.

The next day we rose early because Pancho had medical appointments that he insisted were only routine in nature. After a hearty breakfast filled with loud laughter and more storytelling, Pancho announced that he would be back in another two weeks. "Get ready for an exciting round of golf. We'll bring the course to its knees," he shouted as he stepped out onto our front porch.

When he reached the bottom of the stairs, he turned around to face C.E. and me and laughingly shouted, "I am going to live to be 110 and so will the two of you." He then hopped into his vehicle, leaving only a slight dust trail to remind us he would be back soon. That was the last time we saw Pancho. A few weeks later he was dead from heart related issues. Gone, at the snap of a finger, our friend was no more.

C.E. took Pancho's passing harder than I expected. "We went through so much together, Bonita. I'll miss him always," C.E. said quietly, while tears streamed down both cheeks.

Pancho and C.E. had forged a special friendship that began when C.E. hired him as his company's COO. Even though there was a pause after the asset sale, they came together and forged an even stronger friendship than before.

After Pancho's death, C.E.'s health began to worsen. But, like Pancho, who assured C.E. how great he looked, I told him much the same thing. C.E. had an array of health issues, the key one likely related to stress. It was the opinion of many of our friends that his declining health was brought on in some form or another by the stress he endured during and after his company's asset sale. It was my opinion as well. I saw his demeanor change right after the asset sale. He was never the same person again. And for awhile I was no different. We became lost souls in a world of uncertainty and fear. Like beach sand that washes away with each tide, our lives as we knew them eroded until they disappeared. Dreams were shattered, hearts were broken, and despair consumed us. The idea of getting up to face another day became more sad than joyful.

Never in my wildest dreams did I expect such an ending to our once happy and promising lives. It didn't have to happen the way it did. I can't count how many times over the years I looked back and asked myself, what if I had talked C.E. out of taking the CEO job, what if he had asked my advice when his company's assets were being sold, what if I had said this, what if I had said that….I kicked myself over and over until one day C.E., in his most patient manner, said in his sternest voice yet, "Bonita, shoulda, coulda, woulda, is not something we will talk about any longer. You can't blame yourself for what happened to us. It was the people involved in the asset sale. They didn't keep their word, weren't honest and, frankly, it was my fault for putting too much trust in them and the phony sales process manufactured by the bank."

I learned early in my life that you shouldn't put your trust in anyone. My instincts and intuition have saved me more than once. I only wish I could have conveyed those attributes to C.E.

I wasn't as shocked as C.E. when our turbulent and troubled financial crisis began. From the outset, I had misgivings about whom he was dealing with regarding his company, his career, his future, and mine. I ended up being right, but who wants to be right about something like that? I wish to this day I had been wrong. For a long time, I had recurring nightmares about how things could have ended up differently for those who cheated and deceived C.E. It was as if an alarm clock would go off and I'd wake up in the middle of the night, anxious and sweating from what seemed at the time more a horror film nightmare than a simple dream. It was one filled with violence and destruction. It was like a Godfather movie wipeout moment. I could see a crowd of people I didn't recognize form into a mob. The faceless armed men and women marched to the locations where each of the people involved in the asset sale was enjoying their lives. One by one they were taken down with a variety of weapons, all intended to end their lives—some while having dinner with their families, some carting groceries into their vehicles, others while swimming in their pools, and still others toasting champagne on their yachts. I felt that the phrase *An eye for an eye and a tooth for a tooth* was justified in retaliation for those responsible for our downfall. Yet, in the end, my thoughts rested with words from Matthew 5, *"...which allow for us to love not to hate your enemies and pray for those who persecute you."*

After he lost his company, C.E. pretty much checked out. He spent hours sharpening his wide collection of knives and cleaning his array of antique pistols, choosing to ignore old friends, and protecting himself from making new ones.

It became up to me to find a way out of the unfortunate circumstances that shattered our once bright lives and hurled us into darkness.

I first had to calm myself and get a grip, or suffer a nervous breakdown or, worse, blow out my brains. It was up to me to figure out a way to overcome my paralyzing fright and despair while simultaneously assuring C.E. that he was not responsible for our losses. When not occupied with lifting him up emotionally, I spent the rest of my time figuring out ways to pay all the bills that kept mounting on my desk day after day, month after month, with no end in sight. I constantly thought about how to keep from losing almost everything we had worked for all our lives and how to deal with the incessant calls from creditors. It felt as if the devil had entered every aspect of our being, haunting and tormenting us day and night, while there was no one to call for help. Until, one day, I felt God's presence in our home.

My prayers to God for His mercy began to take hold over time. He heard me. And he responded by showering his grace upon me, C.E., and our lives. I found a couple of consulting jobs that helped alleviate our financial crisis. We developed and stuck to a strict budget that helped to keep us afloat. In time, we were able to settle our debts with lenders by agreeing to payment plans that we could afford. We both came together more loving and caring of each other than ever before. Things were turning around for us.

Then, one day, C.E. hurried out of his closet and said in his go-to manner when something unusual happened, "Shit oh dear, what the hell is this?" pointing to his knees, which were a deep purple. As he took a few steps closer to where I was lying in bed, he pointed to his swollen feet. "What the fuck over!" he shouted.

It took many tests to find the cause of the sudden swelling of his legs and feet. By the time the tests were completed, it was too late. He was in a perilous state of health from heart and auto immune issues which he never recovered. The pandemic didn't help matters. In-person doctor appointments became almost nonexistent, and Zoom calls were almost impossible given our remote residential location. And, since C.E. didn't feel all that bad, he didn't see the medical urgency to pursue more thorough diagnostic treatment.

C.E. didn't talk death. So, we gallantly carried on as if he was going to live forever. Yet I knew he didn't have long. Even though I had time to prepare for C.E.'s passing, there wasn't a quick fix or remedy that released me from the excruciating emotional pain I felt when he passed. Time doesn't matter, you can lose a loved one suddenly or slowly over time. The deep emotional pain of the loss is the same, its immeasurable and indescribable and one that I don't wish on anyone. At times it has brought me to my knees while I did everything in my power to keep from keeling over. It's a pain that I dread when it comes unexpectedly, but one that I will not allow to last forever. Like everything bad that happens in life, I am convinced that this, too, shall pass.

C.E. did his best to remain the same person I met over forty years earlier, yet he was a tormented and dispirited man. He experienced the anguish of losing a company he loved, the loss of a dedicated workforce that supported and cared about him, the loss of just about everything we possessed, and the loss of our financial standing. Perhaps worst of all, however, was the personal and professional attacks to which he was subjected. Maligned by those who bought and sold his company's assets, even his patriotism, military rank, and service to his country was questioned. It sent him into a tailspin of no return. C.E. was a honorable man who did everything he could to cooperate so that the asset sale went smoothly, only to be deceived and maligned by those that participated in his company's asset sale.

At the end of his life, C.E. became so weak he could no longer walk without my assistance. I became his caregiver—the last thing I'd ever thought I'd find myself doing. It became a sad turn of events to see my once strong warrior, protector, and my adviser in all things personal and professional become so physically weak. His mind was sharp as ever but the ship that brought him to this life could no longer function. It was beyond repair, collapsing one piece at a time until it was no more. I'd never witnessed a person's passing, so I had no frame of reference about what to expect from myself. I was terribly conflicted about whether or not I wanted to witness C.E.'s departure. I was afraid I'd have his death scene etched in my mind forever. I remained at his bedside, gently kissing both of his hands, which represented so much of our happy lives together. They were the hands that carried me across the threshold of our first home, the hands that lifted me up when times were hard, the hands that lovingly caressed my face, the hands that poured wine into my glass, and the hands that held his martini, clinking our glasses three times for good luck, and they were the hands that gently held my hands everywhere we stepped out together.

I could go on. I held onto C.E.'s hands until our priest said," He's leaving us," and then added, "He's with God now." It was an experience I will never forget but it's not one that haunts me as I once thought. I didn't want to see C.E. suffer any longer and more than anything in the world, I wanted his mind to be free of all that haunted him for so many years about how he/we came to lose everything, an event that didn't have to happen if people had kept their word.

During one of our last moments together in our kitchen, he put one arm around me while he steadied his other hand on his ever-present walking cane and cried softly, "I am sorry I am leaving you all alone, Bonita. Please forgive me sugar." That was the first and only time he came close to acknowledging that he wouldn't be around much longer.

I held up as best I could throughout C.E.'s memorial service, and thereafter. Friends who lost loved ones warned that one day I would break down and bawl uncontrollably like a baby. It happened one day out of the blue. As much as I tried, I couldn't control the tears. They streamed like a hard rainfall down my checks and down to my chest area where they rested like a tidal pool. I wailed louder than I remembered the old Mexican women in my hometown did when they lost their loved ones, which back then I found to be strange behavior.

Then, suddenly, I seemed to hear my late mother Lola's deep-throated voice from the beyond. *"Bonita, por favor, stop and smell the coffee. Husbands can be replaced, parents and children cannot and guys are a dime a dozen. So, comb your hair, color your lips, get your ass up and stop crying."*

Lola's words not only served to get me out of that paralyzingly sad moment, but they also served to remind me that I was never again going to see the man who rescued me from myself so many years earlier. C.E.'s protective and loving embraces and warm kisses were gone like the wind, his deep sexy baritone voice was only a memory and fading every day. My photographic memory was all that I had left to hold on to our enormously happy times together. I remembered the day we met as if only moments had passed. C.E., accompanied by the Army officer he was to replace in his assignment, walked into the office where I was working. I took one look at the dark curly-haired sexy-looking but shy young Army major and noticed he did pretty much the same of me. *"That was all she wrote,"* C.E. often said of our love at first sight meeting.

Our lives changed that day forever. Never had I been so swept off my feet and, according to C.E., neither had he. The day we met I had recently broken my engagement to a very kind man but one that I wasn't in love with. C.E., however, was married with two children. It took us many years of forging a deep and abiding friendship to realize we could no longer be just friends and pretend that he was married.

One day he sat me down and said in his most serious voice, "I can't and don't want to live one more day without you, Bonita."

It was an exceedingly difficult decision for both of us to make. We didn't want to hurt anyone, but we were at a point in our lives where we had developed such an intense love for one another that it could no longer be ignored. We had to be true to ourselves and to the rest of the world.

I reflected on the fun and magical times we had throughout our marriage, and there was a multitude of them. C.E.'s favorite story, which he told anyone who would listen, was related to his first assignment as a one-star general. The post he reported to had become a retirement assignment to many before him. But in C.E.'s case, it was the stepping stone that made him one of the youngest generals ever assigned to the post. In an assignment at that level, there would generally be people helping to unwrap our household goods and place them in their proper places in our military-assigned home. But, for some reason, C.E. and I ended up unwrapping our household goods. There we stood, me in my cut-off jeans, topped with a Texas Aggie T-shirt, which was a welcome to Texas gift from a friend and my ever-present Sperry Topsiders. C.E. was dressed in his favorite attire—Levi jeans, a polo t-shirt, and cowboy boots. As rock music blared in the background, a middle-aged sergeant representing the Army post's liaison office walked hurriedly into the house, shoved C.E. aside, and yelled, "Outta the way, fella, I'm looking for the general." As he marched down the long hallway, C.E. leaned over and laughingly said, "I don't think he's going to find him down there." The sergeant disappeared down the hall and just as quickly returned and yelled, "Okay, you two, stop playing games and tell me where the fuck is the general?" I looked at him straight in the eye, raised my eyebrows and pointed my eyes toward C.E. The man practically jumped out of his skin and yelled, "Good God Almighty, they're making them younger these days!" All three of us had the laugh of our lives and every time C.E. told the story later in his life, the laughter between us was the same as the day it happened.

One of my favorite memories was when we found ourselves on a nude beach on the French Riviera. Our swimwear made us stand out among the unclothed souls strolling along the beach. It took the two of us only a few seconds to look at each other and laughingly say in unison, "What the hell, when in Rome do as the Romans do."

Then there was the time we visited our California friends, during the Academy awards. We were staying at the same hotel where many of the Oscar nominees, along with many other well-known celebrities, were also staying. The evening prior to the Oscars, the hotel provided a chauffeur-driven car to take us to meet our friends at a nearby restaurant, and as we stepped out of the hotel's rear entrance we were unsuspectedly met by a large roaring crowd. They had gathered to greet the stars staying at the hotel. We could hear one person after another ask, "Who are they?" as they pointed toward us. "Who cares! They must be famous," someone shouted from above the crowd noise as the loud clapping and hand waving continued while C.E. and I happily waved back as if we were "somebodies" from the Hollywood scene.

These days, when I am working outdoors on our small farm, I look for C.E. to be standing on our back deck, the same place where for years we watched endless contrails cover the sky while we happily sipped cocktails and listened to soft jazz tunes from our favorite singer, Diana Krall. I hear C.E.'s whistle, signaling me to come in, while adding a hurried wave that it's time to stop working and join him for dinner. But like a magic show—*poof*—he's disappeared. The deck, except for the table and chairs and the covered outdoor bar that we both designed, is empty of C.E. It's all memories from here on in but, for me, those sweet and enchanting memories will never die.

I was a rebel and hell-raising girl that only a tough but a very patient person like C.E. could tame. He showed me more love and kindness than any one person I've ever known. He was an avid reader of every book imaginable, and he taught me to be still long enough to do the same. Our relationship was built on the trust and on the enormous respect we had for one another. The only time our marriage experienced a few cracks was when his company's assets were sold, but the cracks weren't deep and certainly didn't last long. All in all, we built a truly happy and loving life together. We rarely raised our voices and were true to one another always.

It was a splendid life that I will miss for the rest of my days! We also built a family. Halfway through our marriage, we rescued a Peruvian mother and her young child from an abusive environment. They became part of our family. So much so, we considered them our children and they considered us their parents. I never witnessed C.E. in a happier state than when he was around our two charges, especially the young boy that C.E. was able to watch develop into a remarkable young man, whom he loved deeply and proud to call his son. That young man, in concert with his mother, keep an eye on me, and I couldn't be more blessed to have both in my life. I love both immensely as if they were my own from birth. C.E.'s two children from an earlier marriage were also in our lives. He loved them and I love them too. Each of them, in their own way, reminds me so much of their father, my husband, my best friend, and the absolute love of my life.

My story has no happy ending. Today, I live on the small farm that C.E. and I built together but without my beloved Levy, whom I miss more every day that passes. I live on a fixed income from money saved by C.E. throughout his military career. It is money he earned from years of serving his country honorably, not from money that he got by cheating and stealing from others.

As I said earlier, dark times will likely occur in everyone's life. It's how we handle the situation that is the crux of this book. So, not unlike the time we lost our financial standing, I not only worked tirelessly day in and day out to cope, and comfort C.E., but also to encourage, console, and comfort myself. These days, I have only myself to be concerned about and that's a lonely track indeed. Except I recently added a puppy toy poodle to my life that is helping me transition from being C.E.'s wife to being his widow and to being a new mother.

Even though I feel like I am an old hand at dealing with losses, losing a loved one has a whole different meaning on so many levels– in the words of the late Queen Elizabeth, "Grief is the price we pay for love." The anxiety and depression over C.E.'s loss comes in waves. One day I'll be fine but, on another day, the emotional pain can bring me to my knees, sobbing uncontrollably and unable to steady myself. Thankfully, I have my yoga mat to lie down on and meditate until the pain is lessened, the tears stop falling, and the anxiety is reduced. I've come to learn that the emotional pain I endured when we lost our financial standing was a cakewalk compared to the pain I am experiencing from losing the love of my life. It's an ass kicker!

I work every day to be a kinder and more gentle soul and not be consumed with what happened to our financial and personal lives. I no longer question why I came to lose C.E. Instead, I take time every day to thank God for His grace and blessings. My faith in God has become stronger. I believe that God gives us our abilities, our strengths, and his protection. He answers our prayers. God always saves us in the end. I live in a world without C.E. with those spiritual words in mind. His memory will live on, but at the same time, the world doesn't stop because of his passing. The earth continues turning on its axis, the sun rises and sets as always, the lives of others continue, and so will my life. In the words of the famous French painter, Francoise Gilot, "You always survive if you think you should." A part of me went with C.E., but the rest of me is looking forward to the next phase of my life. Life is full of surprises, and I am eager to discover what they might be.

For as long as I can remember, Grandma Moses's words, "Life is what you make it, always has been, always will be," have been a mainstay throughout my life. It's up to us how our story ends, not others.

That girl, full of grit and grace, is back!

Made in the USA
Middletown, DE
17 June 2023

32178321R00116